CHAPTER ONE

THE WATERY British sun, on this summer day of 1815, shone in between wine velvet draperies pulled back from the second-storey window of a bachelors' rooming-house on Jermyn Street. Weak as the light was, it showed up the faint lines of dissipation beginning to mar the excessively handsome features of the dark-haired young gentleman seated at a breakfast of rare beef and ale.

Mr. Robert Merrivale Greenwood, Corinthian, member of the Fair-in-Hand Club and of Gentleman Jackson's saloon, and a fencer of some skill, had come upon a perplexing problem. He shoved askew the brocade silk cap that matched his floral-patterned dressing robe, the better to scratch above one ear. It didn't help. He stretched out his long legs and recrossed his elegantly shod ankles, his gleaming Hessians reflecting a beam of the sunshine. This didn't help, either.

The letter he perused was from his solicitor. He read it again, turning it over and over as if some solution to its puzzle could be found on its other side. None could. Apparently, if he wished to learn why the man had to see him at once, there was naught to do but visit him. Mr. Robert Greenwood owned a strong bump of curiosity.

An hour later, he was on his way to Lincoln's Inn in his curricle, a light, two-wheeled racing vehicle drawn by a pair of high-stepping chestnuts. He cut a magnificent figure in his many-caped driving coat, handling his pair like a master whip, weaving his way through the crowded streets of London, narrowly missing hawkers, hand-cart peddlers and slow-moving drays.

From his French father he had inherited curly black hair, liquid dark eyes and classic features that might have bordered on beauty had he not carefully cultivated an ironic twist to his sculpted lips and a supercilious lift to his brows. He was considered by the matrons of the ton to be a rake and an inveterate here-and-there-ian, one against whom their daughters must be guarded at all costs. This circumstance suited him, for at not yet thirty, he had no intention of becoming leg-shackled for many years to come.

A devil-may-care driver, he took a corner in style, showing off his skill, and the next moment he was battling to control his rearing pair.

Their hooves flailed inches above the head of a young woman who had stepped onto the road. A large hatbox, knocked from her hands, spilled a brilliantly coloured bonnet into the dirt, and the lady screamed, not for herself but for the hat.

Robert's horses once more on all four feet, he threw his reins to his groom and leapt to the rescue, pushing aside a delighted gaggle of lookers-on.

She was down on one knee, her skirts draggled in the dust as she gathered up the bonnet, scattered sheets of silver paper, the hatbox and its lid.

"Madam," Robert exclaimed, "I pray you are not injured!" He caught her arm and attempted to drag her to her feet.

She shook him off, eyes blazing. "No! Though not through any fault of yours. Cow-handed cawker! Can you not control your beasts?"

Affronted, Robert stood back. He considered himself an expert whip, quite top-o'-the-trees. Ask anyone in London! As for fault, why had she not looked where she was going?

"The roads, madam," he informed her stiffly, "are for carriages. One expects pedestrian travellers to keep an eye out for traffic."

"Traffic? Is that what you call racing higgeldy-piggeldy down the thoroughfare and round the corners without a thought or glance to whom you might run down?"

She had retrieved her belongings and now stood with the garish bonnet in her hands, meticulously examining every petal of its trimming for possible damage. The hat was an atrocious affair in Robert's opinion, the chip-straw brim decorated with an oversize wreath of red silk roses and green leaves. The leaves sparkled with cut-glass dewdrops, and each rose held a huge pearl at its centre, which seemed to him a vulgar display.

The lady, who had been ignoring him, now chose to recognize his presence once more.

"It is not seriously damaged, thank goodness, but no thanks to you." She had by now taken in his impeccable Town rig and the elegance of his curricle and pair. Her delicate lip curled. "You must know, I have the lowest opinion of useless parasites on society who have no thought but their own pleasure and no consideration for others."

Robert could see no earthly reason why he must know this, but he had no chance of rebuttal. With a final glare from her remarkably fine grey eyes and a toss of fashionably styled brown curls, she tenderly replaced her bonnet in its box and stalked off. The crowd dispersed and Robert, rather amused, climbed back into his curricle and proceeded on his way. Females and their gewgaws! There was no understanding them. Demmed pretty girl, though.

HIS CURIOSITY still piqued, Robert bounded up the dark, narrow stairway to his solicitor's rooms on the second floor. He flung open the door without knocking.

The startled clerk in the anteroom rose from behind his lecturnlike desk in some confusion.

"He wants to see me," Robert informed the man casually, and pressed on through to the inner sanctum marked Private.

Mr. Breckenridge, the solicitor, a thin man with thin lips, thinning hair and a dry sense of humour, observed his entrance calmly. He had handled Robert's affairs since the death of the boy's parents when Robert was very young, and the two were on easy terms.

"Pray be seated, my lord," he greeted Robert, shuffling a pile of papers into a neat stack on his desk. "Surely, such tumultuous behaviour is unnecessary."

Robert sank into one of the leather chairs, believing his elevation to the peerage to be one of the man's attempts at levity. He responded in kind.

"May I ask, your worship, why I am summoned to appear in the dock?" It was a few moments before he noticed that the dry smile usually meeting his sallies was noticeably absent.

Breckenridge steepled his fingers and eyed Robert thoughtfully over them. "Tell me, my boy," he began, "what do you know of your family?"

"Why, you know as much as I. My mother was a cousin of Lord Merrivale's."

"I refer to your father."

Robert shrugged. There was very little he knew of his paternal parent, other than that he had come from France at the beginning of the Reign of Terror. "The family did not approve of my mother marrying a penniless *émigré*. I do not even know his real name. He had adopted the English Greenwood before I was born, and the change was accepted by my grandfather."

Mr. Breckenridge massaged his chin. "Have you never wondered why?"

Robert grinned. "I have oft-times wondered if he was escaping from the law. It was only their love for my mother that caused the Merrivales to take me in after my parents' deaths. His name was never again mentioned."

Breckenridge tapped his finger on the sheaf of papers. "Have you never thought the change might have been for his safety—and yours?"

Robert's eyes narrowed. "Whatever are you getting at, sir?"

"Translate your name into French," the solicitor ordered patiently.

"Greenwood—green forest? *Bois vert?*"

Breckenridge nodded. "Unlikely as it may seem," he told Robert, "you are now the Comte de Boisvert."

"Good God!" said Robert inadequately.

"Your father," Breckenridge continued, "was the younger son of the old *comte*. The elder brother died in the Terror without a legitimate heir. The old man went into hiding and survived to reclaim his estate by swearing allegiance to Napoleon. He recently passed from this vale of tears and his executors have traced you down. I received these papers only last evening."

"Good God," said Robert again, stunned as the reality sank in.

"I have here a copy of Boisvert's will, which I understand is being read to the family today. It is a somewhat peculiar document."

He coughed, a very dry cough, leafed through the papers, and selected one. "This is a careful translation, which I am directed to read to you as the others are hearing it today in France."

He started on the legal terms and Robert held up a hand. "Never mind the formal jargon. Cut line, Breck. Give me the gist without roundaboutation."

Breckenridge eyed him, a bit in a huff. No doubt he was proud of his translation. He sighed. "Youth," he remarked. "Ever impetuous. Very well, here it is, then. The title goes to you—that could not be changed—but the rest of the estate is not entailed and was the old *comte*'s to dispose of as he would.''

He rattled the papers in his hand and looked at Robert over the top of his steel-rimmed spectacles. ''The will states that he desired to re-establish the Boisvert bloodline where it belongs. On the Continent, not in England. There is only one other legitimate heir, one Étienne de Boisvert, a cousin and contemporary of the late *comte,* who unfortunately has no children to carry on the family name. To remedy this, the old *comte* laid down some definite provisos.''

He hunted for and found another page. ''There is a vast estate involved. It will all go to you if you fulfil a few simple requirements. First you must marry the *comte*'s great-niece, the last female of the direct line—''

Here Robert interrupted. ''Marry? Me? You're bamming!''

''Not at all. I quite understand the man's desire to perpetuate his blood and his name. Next, you must leave at once for France, and reside in the Château de Boisvert for at least six months of each year. If you fail in this, the elderly cousin will prevail, and the name of Boisvert in France will be no more.''

Robert heard only one phrase—he was expected to go to France.

He couldn't believe his ears. Old Breck knew of his problem! His stomach lurched and he swallowed hard, for the otherwise redoubtable Robert had an Achilles' heel—an ingrained terror of water. His fear was justified. As a small boy he had nearly drowned in the boating accident that killed his parents. Unconscious when dragged from the sea, he had barely survived and still bore an invisible wound. Even a brief excursion on the Thames occasioned violent seasickness, and his only attempt to visit Vauxhall with a water party had led to embarrassing consequences. The thought of crossing the Channel to France left him white faced and weak in the knees. He shuddered. The mere mention of a sea voyage brought on a wave of the wrenching horror and utter desolation of a seven-year-old child suddenly and traumatically bereft of both father and mother.

"No," he said flatly.

Mr. Breckenridge shook his head. "I suggest that you go, Robert. It is time and more that you settle down and give up your life of foolish larks and gaming. It has come to my notice that you have shown no desire to fix your interest with any damsel of your acquaintance. Here you are offered an excellent marriage of convenience, including a vast estate. You would be a fool to whistle such a match down the wind.''

''I am not setting foot on a boat!''

''Then you had best swim.'' Breckenridge patted his arm, kindly refraining from mentioning the rough water to be encountered on the Channel at this time of year. ''Robert, my boy, it is time you faced this cowardly fear of the water.''

Cowardly! Robert's head snapped up. No man had ever called him a coward, nor would one have the chance! His stomach churned at the idea, but he vowed to cross the Channel if it killed him—which he feared it might.

AT DAWN, Miss Elizabeth Garner stood on the quay in Dover, buffeted by a freshening wind, and tasting the salt on her lips. Sea birds circled overhead with raucous squawks, hawsers creaked as the boats still in the basin rose and fell, tiny wavelets slapping against their hulls. On the dock around her, workmen ran to and fro, heaving aboard final loadings, for the early tide had to be caught. Many ships had sailed already—including the packet for France.

Elizabeth drew in despairing lungfuls of briny air as it sailed away without her. At the last moment, she had panicked and run back down the gangway, a bandbox clutched in one arm and a large hatbox swinging from the other by its looped cord. On her head was the bonnet it usually contained, a spectacular creation with a chip-straw brim and the crown wreathed in a mass of red silk roses and green leaves, all appearing to be slightly damp from recent washing.

She watched the diminishing sails of the packet, beset by second thoughts—now, when it was too late. How could she have done so foolish a thing? After hours of arguing with herself, stewing and shilly-shallying, she had finally come to the great decision to marry her third cousin once-removed, Andrew Belmont. And then what had she done? Like an absolute ninny, she had run away before reaching point-non-plus.

But she *had* to marry Andrew. It had not been an easy matter to decide; then the death of the aunt with whom she had lived since becoming an orphan at an early age left her without family, and an unmarried maiden could not live alone. She had turned down several respectable offers, waiting for the dream of every young miss, but true love had not come her way, and she was quite on the shelf, being now five-and-twenty. Andrew was the least of known evils.

There was nothing for it but to stop this foolishness and find other passage to France, for Andrew awaited her at Calais. He had only the one day in which to meet her, marry her and carry her off with him to Vienna, where he was to attend the Peace Congress as a member of General Lord Cathcart's staff.

Mayhew, her abigail, had gone aboard the packet, seeing to the stowing of Elizabeth's trunks in one of the cabins. No doubt she was still below deck and had no idea her charge would have to take another ship, and alone. What would Andrew say when he found out? Oddly, Elizabeth was more concerned about the trimming she would receive from Mayhew when she finally arrived in France.

She had no fear of being unable to locate Andrew once she reached Calais. Having a genuine aptitude for languages, she spoke excellent French and could ask questions easily.

But now they were questions in English, directed to the most elderly and honest-appearing of the men on the waterfront, which led her to a sleek schooner, heaving gently at the dockside, the grey water lapping at its sides. The owner, a solid, weathered man with side whiskers, leaned stolidly against a stack of kegs. He looked up from overseeing the loading of a final bale of goods as she approached.

"Do you take passengers?" she asked. "I must get to France at once."

He straightened, looking her over with a considering eye. Elizabeth flushed, knowing what he must have been thinking, for no lady of Quality travelled alone. ''I have only just missed the packet,'' she explained. ''My abigail and all my luggage are on it and I must meet the boat in Calais.''

He studied her expensive travelling cloak of blue-and-green-tartan Scottish wool, worn over a neat, dark blue merino gown of simple design. The bonnet gave him a moment's pause. He scratched the tip of his nose. ''Have ye the blunt for your fare?''

''Certainly. That is, how much?''

She had just completed negotiations for her passage across the channel when a hackney disgorged a tall young man carrying a portmanteau. He marched towards them with an arrogant, even challenging, swing to his stride as though daring the world to judge him. His face was set, his jaw jutting with determination as he came up to them. Elizabeth recognized the rackety gentleman who had nearly run her down the day before.

He also recognized her, or rather her new bonnet, for he muttered, ''Good God, that hat again.''

He then turned and addressed the ship's captain. ''My name is Greenwood. I understand you have the fastest boat from here to France. I want to book passage on her, for I wish to spend as little time as possible in crossing the Channel.''

Elizabeth glared at his back. "Sir, I have just chartered this vessel. You must find another."

He barely gave her an abstracted glance. "Captain, I am in no mood to argue. I want the fastest ship and I am told this is it. Name your price."

"My dear sir!" Elizabeth expostulated.

The captain, however, eyed the gentleman speculatively. "What's your hurry, cully? One step ahead of the duns—or the law?"

The man lost patience. "Neither. What must it be, passage or purchase?"

Elizabeth stared wide-eyed as he pulled a heavy pouch from his pocket and began to count out golden coins. What an addle-pated thing to do! He was asking to be robbed. How fortunate that he intended to leave this port at once!

He quickly came to terms with the captain and turned back to her. "Sorry, miss. This ship is now mine."

"In that case," she declared, standing her ground, "I am your passenger, Mr. Greenwood. I have paid my way."

He shrugged, an almost Gallic gesture. "Then get on board. Neither the tide nor I can wait."

The captain gestured to a sailor, who took up Miss Garner's bandbox. She followed him up the gangplank and onto the schooner's deck.

After a moment's hesitation, the young man squared his shoulders, took a deep breath and strode in their wake.

The captain picked his teeth as he watched them, a calculating gleam in his eye.

IT WAS NOT SO BAD at first. Robert stood in the bow, the fresh wind in his face. The lady had stowed her bonnet in its box, it being in danger of blowing from her head, and she remained on deck beside him. Why, he wondered, would one who speaks like a gentlewoman travel alone and sport so vulgar a headpiece? He stole glances now and again, for she was an intriguing sight with her garments flattened against her body by the wind and her soft brown hair flying about her face, loosened from its pins. The wind whipped her skirt about her limbs, but, a minor disappointment, the weighted hem of her petticoat preserved her modesty.

She did not hold Robert's interest long, for they were soon clear of the Tidal Harbour and entered upon the open Channel. A following sea rocked the ship unevenly from side to side and bow to stern. Robert gazed in dismay at the heaving grey water flecked with foam. In a very short time, he began to suspect he had erred in selecting a smaller, faster boat to ferry him across the choppy Channel.

Somewhere he recalled hearing that the larger the ship, the less rolling and pitching. Too late.

The schooner lifted her bow sharply over the trough of a wave and plunged sickeningly downward. Summoning what dignity he could muster under the circumstances, Robert addressed the lady.

"Miss, I must beg you to look the other way. I fear," he explained carefully, "I am about to be excessively unwell." He headed for the rail.

Elizabeth's sympathy, always easily aroused, came to the fore. An excellent sailor herself, she had aided others and knew the necessary procedure. Snatching off her warm cloak, she draped it over Robert's shaking shoulders and sent one of the amused sailors for a basin of water and a towel. Between his bouts of miserable retching, she mopped her companion's perspiring brow.

Luckily, a strong off-shore wind filled the billowing sails, and the schooner alternately dived through the waves and skimmed others like one of the sea birds. It should be a short crossing, Elizabeth thought. Far better for Mr. Greenwood, in his delicate condition, to be tossed about by the sea for only four hours or less than to make a calmer trip that might mean a full day of the gentle rise, hesitation and sudden drop, over and over, of a near-windless day. Even so, she began to wonder if the poor man would make it to solid ground.

Long hours passed. Far too many for a Channel crossing. When a faint ribbon of land at last came into view on the horizon, Elizabeth drew a deep breath of relief. She went in search of the captain, finding him at last standing in the bow, watching the passing shore of France and blowing a cloud from an evil-smelling cigar, fortunately to the lee of Mr. Greenwood, who had troubles enough.

"How much longer before we arrive at Calais?" she asked.

"Calais? We do not arrive there."

"What can you mean? Of course we go to Calais. I have purchased my passage to that destination!"

The captain grinned. "The gentleman purchased my boat, and Mr. Greenwood's orders are to go to the Bay of Boisvert, on the southern coast."

Elizabeth stared at him, aghast. "But I must be in Calais by nightfall!"

He casually tossed the stub of his cigar over the rail. "I suggest you take this matter up with the owner of the boat."

"You must know he is in no condition to discuss anything!"

The man shrugged, dismissing her. "Mayhap you can find ground transport from Boisvert to Calais. I wish you luck, ma'am."

Furious, she returned to Mr. Greenwood. He still hung halfway over the stern rail, and she forcibly resisted an urge to push him the rest of the way into the sea.

Matters became worse. Some hours later, she looked around and saw that one of the sailors had opened her bandbox and was rummaging through it.

"Here, what do you think you are doing?" she cried. "Stop that—stop..."

Her voice trailed away. She faced the black hole of the muzzle of a pistol, in the hands of the captain.

CHAPTER TWO

A RABBIT MESMERIZED by a snake, Elizabeth stared at the black mouth of the pistol. Robert Greenwood hung helpless over the rail.

"Sir!" She reached behind her, felt about, and grabbed his arm. "Do something!"

"I am," he managed to gasp out.

"I mean, something *else*." Her voice quavered. "I believe we are going to die."

"Thank God," he croaked, and cast up his accounts once more.

The evil captain grunted. "If you prefer to live a little longer, you will hand over your money and your jewels. But I can, of course, shoot you first."

This welcome suggestion caught Robert's attention. "Go ahead. Shoot," he begged. "Be quick about it."

"Really!" Elizabeth exclaimed. "You are no better than a bacon-brained clodpoll!"

He moaned. "Must you mention bacon?"

Behind the menacing captain, a bustle of activity began. Two of his men had raised the sail on a tiny dinghy and were lowering it over the side with ropes. It hit the water with a splash.

Elizabeth gazed at the scene in horror. "Surely you do not mean to cast us adrift! You must put us ashore!"

Never before had she seen so wolfish a grin. The captain's teeth were discoloured and uneven. She found herself staring in fascination at his one gold incisor and the empty space next to it. She pulled her eyes away. "You cannot do this," she exclaimed.

The grin widened, displaying another space. "The gentleman's orders were to take him to the Bay of Boisvert. That's it ahead. No need for the rest of us to make a landing."

"Mr. Greenwood—" Elizabeth shook the seasick man's arm, and he turned a haggard face. "They are putting us off the ship!"

"Good," he gasped. "Anything is better than this."

One of the men grabbed Elizabeth from behind and pushed her roughly towards the side where the little sailboat bobbed, still held by the ropes. A hemp ladder was hanging over the rail, and the man gestured for her to climb down.

"I cannot!"

"Would you rather," the captain asked, "have the gentleman go first an' cop a dekko up your skirts while you descend?"

Elizabeth looked about wildly for help. The boatmen were enjoying themselves hugely, as though the whole affair were a party. Mr. Greenwood had draped himself once more over the rail, and one of the men had taken her precious bonnet from the box. He minced around the deck with it on his head to roars of laughter from his mates.

"Oh!" she cried. "My new bonnet! Oh, please, give it back." Her face puckered and a tear of frustration ran down her cheek.

A kinder soul than the others snatched it from his mate's head and tossed it to her. She caught it up and pressed it against her bosom, ignoring the possible detriment to the roses. Gathering up some of the scattered silver paper and the hatbox, and finally finding the lid, she stuffed her bonnet back inside.

The man who had retrieved it for her helped her over the side and steadied the rope-ladder as she negotiated the swinging rungs, the hatbox slung over her arm by its loops. Mr. Greenwood, weak and shaky, made it halfway down and fell the last few feet into the bottom of the little boat, nearly capsizing it.

MINUS ELIZABETH'S BANDBOX, her pearl necklet and the heavy pouch from Robert's coat pocket, they sat alone in the small sailboat, cast off from the schooner, which was already disappearing in a mist that gathered around them. That is, Elizabeth sat, clutching her hatbox; Robert lay in the bottom of the boat, covered by her cloak. He was not in the best of moods.

"That damned hat," he complained weakly. "Vanity, thy name is woman. Why could you not have used your tears to beg them to put us ashore instead of leaving us adrift in this devilish Channel?"

Elizabeth did not deign to answer. She had *not* shed tears. Well, perhaps one, but there had been provocation.

The sail flapped idly in the light breeze, and she looked at what seemed a welter of ropes and pulleys. "Can you sail, sir?"

"Of course not," he replied.

She was not to be discouraged. "No matter. We are within sight of land, and do look! There is a boat putting out! They will rescue us."

"If they find us."

"How could they not? We are right here. Oh, no!" she exclaimed, anguished. "They do not come our way—they are heading for that tiny island."

Scrambling to her feet, she clung to the mast with one arm and waved the other frantically. Her sudden action rocked the boat and Robert groaned.

"Help me shout," she ordered. "We must make them hear us."

Robert pulled himself up on one elbow and peered over the side. "They are too far away."

Not only far away. Even as Elizabeth called and waved, the shoreline, the island and the other boat grew dim and hazy. The breeze had died down and the light mist rapidly became a fog, soon becalming them in a blanket of white.

"Oh," Elizabeth wailed. "They will never find us now. We shall drift here forever." She turned on Robert, forgetting he was too weak to defend himself. "This is all your fault, Mr. Greenwood!"

"*My* fault?"

"Certainly, you brought this upon us by letting that odious man see your money."

He didn't reply, having long since reached the stage of agonizing dry paroxysms that left him so spent that he could barely move, let alone argue with a distraught female.

"I should have asked for food and water. I am hungry," Elizabeth murmured with a wistful sigh. "I had no time to breakfast. Ham...buttered eggs...a muffin and a cup of hot chocolate..."

Robert dragged himself to the edge of the boat again.

"Oh, dear, I *am* sorry." She turned away until the distressing sounds ceased and he settled weakly back.

She thought of another grievance. "I wished to go to Calais, not this...this wherever it is."

"You didn't say so," he told her wearily.

"I took it for granted that Calais would be our port, since it is the nearest to Dover."

"You should have spoken." He thought a moment. "Not that I would have changed my plans. It is essential that I go to Boisvert." He turned his face away and closed his eyes. He opened them again, for without fixing his gaze on the unmoving white above him, he felt the gentle rocking of the boat become more noticeable. "Go away," he added.

"You must know I cannot."

"Then do not complain. You chose to come. I did not invite you along."

About to reply sharply, Elizabeth looked at his haggard features and was overcome by guilt. She was taking unfair advantage of a very ill man. If only there were some way she could help. She lapsed into silence.

The fog thickened until she could no longer see the top of the mast. The small boat drifted, lulling her into a doze. Even Mr. Greenwood finally slept.

Elizabeth sat up suddenly. Odd irregular sounds penetrated the fog. Splashing echoed the gentle lap of the waves against their boat. Something came nearer. A shark? She had heard they were known to attack small boats, imagining them to be enemies. Her heart began to pound and she looked about for a weapon. Oh, what good was a boat without strong oars or even a belaying-pin?

A dim shape appeared in the opaque fog not far from them. Louder splashes indicated someone had seen them and was trying to approach.

"À moi!" a frantic voice shouted. *"Sauvez-moi!"*

Not a shark—perhaps even help. Elizabeth shouted back, "Here! This way!"

A cockleshell of a rowboat, propelled by a man using his hands to paddle, heaved into sight. The man was making little progress. Elizabeth found a loose rope in the bottom of the dinghy and, after several tries, managed to throw it into the rowboat, where it landed safely. Unfortunately, she had forgotten to secure her end.

"Oh, botheration!" she exclaimed.

The paddler beamed. "It is no matter, *mademoiselle*. You will see. I fix."

He did this by tying one end firmly about his waist and rolling the rest into a ball, which he threw to Elizabeth. It unrolled as it went, and she caught her end only by plunging her arms into the water and grabbing at it as it sank. Between them, Elizabeth reeling in and the man clinging to the sides of his boat and pushing his feet against the bow, they managed to bring the little rowboat up to the side, where Elizabeth tied it securely. She extended an eager hand and helped the small, damp Frenchman to scramble across. The sudden rocking of the sailboat wakened Robert. He groaned and dived for the rail.

Elizabeth greeted the newcomer with relief. "My dear sir, can you by any chance be a sailor?"

"But of a certainty, *mademoiselle*." He looked about. "Which rope does one pull to drive this sailship?"

"Oh!" The word was a bitter cry of disappointment. "You are not a sailor at all!"

The Frenchman attempted a bow and grabbed for the support of the mast. "Not as yet, perhaps, but I become whatever so lovely a lady desires," he assured her. "I am your slave, your—"

Elizabeth tried to stamp her foot. "You—you are as impossible as he is!"

The Frenchman took this as a compliment. He bowed again, this time successfully, and kissed her fingertips with true Continental grace.

"But indeed, yes, *mademoiselle*. I am *formidable, incroyable*. Only try me. Give me the task, any under the sun—" he spread his hands dramatically "—or whatever, for it seems the sun has deserted us in this fog."

Elizabeth felt ready to weep, but she was no watering-pot. One must make the best of things, and this little man would be better than nothing.

"I do not know how to handle this boat," she said. "As you see, my companion—" she pointed at Robert's back as he still hung overboard "—is of no earthly—or waterly—use in his condition. I fear he is in very queer stirrups."

"Ah." The Frenchman gave a knowledgeable nod. *"Le mal de mer!"* He rubbed his hands together and reached for one of the lines. "Never fear, I will get us to shore."

He pulled the rope loose.

It hissed through his hands and the boom, released, swung wildly across the boat. They saw it coming and ducked. Robert chose that moment to straighten up. It struck him squarely in the back, knocking him overboard into the black sea.

ROBERT'S WORST nightmare came true. Sheer, mindless terror engulfed him. The dark, heavy water closed over his head, shutting off all light and air. Imaginary denizens of the deep dragged at his legs, holding him under. The sudden icy cold froze his chest, cramping his stomach. Lungs bursting, he struck out madly, breaking to the surface, choking and spluttering.

His eyes were filled with stinging salt, blinding him. Only a mouthful of water kept him from screaming and disgracing himself.

One flailing arm hit something hard. Clawing hands seized him, and he fought hysterically to tear free, but they managed to pull him back into the boat.

He crouched in the bottom, clinging to one of the seats, his teeth chattering as he watched his curly-brimmed beaver float away and disappear in the fog.

"I...can't...swim," he explained, feeling a complete fool now that he was safe.

"Not swim?" exclaimed the Frenchman. "Any person can swim. It is only to hold up one's nose, pretend to be the dog and chase the cat through the water."

This was no time for cats and dogs. Robert roused enough to glare at the Frenchman. "What the devil were you up to, anyway?"

"Now, now," said Elizabeth, attempting to soothe. "He merely tried to help."

"Help!"

She turned away, her attention on attempting to secure the boom. "Why, my dear sir, only a short while ago you *wished* to die."

Robert could think of no adequate riposte. One was not at one's best when seasick.

He was soaked, but he refused to take off his wet clothing with a lady present. The Frenchman finally divested him of his upper garments but Robert would not allow his breeches to be removed.

"You will have then *le zizi très froid*," the Frenchman argued. "It is not a part fond of the cold."

Robert glanced quickly at the lady, but she was attempting to drape his coat and shirt over the bow seat and apparently did not hear. Or perhaps she did not understand. Not everyone spoke French. He rolled himself up in her woollen cloak and lay in the bottom of the boat, shivering.

Elizabeth soon began to be seriously concerned for the poor man. The cold, coupled with his illness, had left him grey faced and hollow eyed. She didn't really like him, but now, seeing him so helpless, she felt all maternal and protective. It touched her heart to see one so virile and arrogant brought to such a state. He might die of an inflammation of the lungs if they did not soon reach shore!

"Have you any idea where we are?" she asked their new companion.

"But of course, *mademoiselle*. We are afloat off the coast of France."

Elizabeth was not to be put off. "Where are we?" she asked, forcing herself to be patient. "Is that truly the Bay of Boisvert—" She started to point in the direction she thought land lay and stopped, dismayed. Fog, a layer of quilt batting, sealed them in.

She had no notion which way they faced. Could the boat have turned when she secured the Frenchman's craft? Or while they hauled Mr. Greenwood back on board? Without the wind at their backs as before, she had absolutely no way of telling north from south. They could be drifting in circles or even towards the open sea. There was naught to do but ride out the fog and hope.

They huddled in the bottom of the boat. There was very little room, for Robert's long legs took up most of the space. A dreary silence settled over them, broken only by Robert's convulsive swallows and occasional moans. Nevertheless, Elizabeth prepared to make the best of it. Well-bred and with a strong social conscience, she attempted to lighten the atmosphere with polite conversation.

"No doubt," she began, "you are wondering how this gentleman, with whom I have no previous acquaintance, and I came to be becalmed in this small boat in the middle of this fog."

The Frenchman also had excellent manners. "Indeed, *mademoiselle,* I have thought no further than to thank *le bon Dieu* that you are here to rescue me."

"I fear you are hardly rescued. You have merely been joined with us in our calamity." She saw he waited for an explanation he was too polite to request, and to be sure one was owed him. Or perhaps, one was owed for *her,* it being a most compromising situation.

"It was quite by accident," she told the Frenchman. "Due to an unfortunate incident on the dock in England—" she couldn't hold back a sulphurous glance at Mr. Greenwood "—the boatmen had reason to fancy us wealthy. We were robbed and cast adrift."

"But, *mademoiselle!*" he exclaimed, delighted. "A—how do you say?—coincidence! So it is with me. Although a difference," he amended. "I am not robbed as yet but am in the greatest danger, and I was not cast adrift by my villains but have so cast myself."

She must have appeared completely mystified, for he hastened on.

"First you must know I am one Armand Brunot. But for a small technicality, I should be the next Comte de Boisvert."

Robert shook his dripping hair from his face. He stared at the little man. "How is this?" he demanded.

Far from reticent, the outspoken Frenchman became expansive, candidly revealing his story.

"*De cette manière.* My father, the heir of the Comte de Boisvert, neglected to marry my mother."

Robert released the breath he held and subsided. He looked the little man over with interest. Was he, then, a relative of a sort? A cousin?

"He was a victim of the Reign of Terror," Armand continued. "Without doubt, a hindrance to his good intentions. My mother was a maid in the château."

Fascinated, Elizabeth questioned him. "But how came you into this current bumble-broth?"

"I search for treasure!" He beamed at her. "The old *comte, mon grand-père,* is now not of this world. His funeral was yesterday, and *mon oncle*—the brother of my mother, you understand, not of the old *comte*—was at last at liberty to speak to me the words of my mother on her deathbed. These words he was sworn not to reveal until the Terror was at an end and the *comte* secured beneath the ground."

He paused dramatically. "He is now safely interred, and *mon oncle* repeats to me her words, a clue to the finding of a treasure left to me by my father. Upon hearing the message, I set out at once to follow her instructions. I start in a boat found for me by one Dupont, who insists on helping me search. But to my misfortune, this Dupont tells M. Gérard, the boat master, my reason for the sail to l'*Île du Renard,* the Island of the Fox, and this Gérard, he wished at once to discover my hoard for himself. When he heard of so great riches, he joined with this knave Dupont, and they planned to drown me farther out at sea."

"It was not very long-headed of you to confide in anyone," chided Elizabeth. "A treasure hunt! No wonder those evil men were tempted. But if they meant to drown you, why did they put you in a boat?"

"Ah, that they did not! I foil them," he declared with pride. "I save myself." Folding his arms across his chest, he sat back, waiting for her admiration.

Elizabeth could no more fail him than she could turn away an eager puppy. "Oh, you must tell me at once!" she exclaimed, clapping her hands. "What did you do?"

"The fog closes in and they become much confused, uncertain which way to go and afraid of running aground on my island, the fog being so solid that one could not see from one end of the boat to the other. While both peer ahead from the bow, I escape in the *bateau,* that rowboat. It is a small matter, but the need for oars does not occur to me until I push off from the ship.''

''I see.'' Elizabeth maintained a straight face. She foresaw a problem. ''But we are stuck here. Will not the villains reach your treasure first?''

''Ah, but they will not find it. I do not have the complete trust in Dupont that you have assumed. I am clever, me. I draw up a false map, and show it to him. Most fortunately, this *cochon* Gérard steals it from me, and may they dig in the sand forever.''

''It is buried then? A chest of gold or jewels?''

''As to that I cannot say. I myself do not know for what I search.''

Elizabeth blinked. ''But how do you mean to find something if you do not know what it is?''

''I will know, will I not, when I follow the clues of my mother and find my treasure? Possibly it is a cache of jewels secreted for safe keeping by my father during the Terror. At least that is what I believe.''

A gentle breeze had begun to lick at the slack sail as they talked. Stiffening, it became a light wind, and the fog began to break up into patches. Elizabeth, looking past Armand, caught a glimpse through a clear space of a grey mound on the horizon.

"Sir," she cried, catching one of Robert's feet and jiggling it to get his attention. "Mr. Greenwood, I can see land!"

Roused from a near stupor, Robert struggled to a sitting position and looked wildly around. "Where?"

The fog thinned more. The narrow strip of coastline lay still covered; only the grey mound, shrouded in mist, was visible.

"That is my island," Armand observed. "But it is now far behind us and grows smaller."

They were drifting the wrong way.

"Oh!" exclaimed Elizabeth. "We must do something!"

Robert was suddenly galvanized into action. "This island, it is solid land?"

"*Mais naturellement!* What would you?"

"Then let us go there. At once." He threw aside the cloak and pulled his wet shirt on over his head.

"Ah," said the Frenchman. "There is nothing I should like more. To whom belongs this ship?"

"Me."

"Then it is you who can sail us?"

Elizabeth explained matters while Robert compressed his lips and stared at the lessening fog.

"If you are completely finished, my dear ma'am," he said, when she and Armand had thrashed out the situation between them, "may I suggest we try to learn how one steers this boat?"

They did not know how to fill the sail, and the rudder made no change without the power of the wind. Robert and the Frenchman studied the ship, tracing the ropes to the flapping sail and discovering the contrariness of the rudder. Armand also discovered that carelessly piled lines could trip someone equally careless, and nearly went overboard like Robert.

"Merde!" he exclaimed, grabbing the rail to save himself.

"I beg your pardon?" said Elizabeth, who was struggling to control the swooping boom. "I cannot cope with French right now. You must speak English if I am to understand you."

He mopped his brow in relief, and Elizabeth wondered if she had heard his word aright after all.

Robert had no such uncertainty. He was fluent in the language of the gutter, having had the benefit of an eloquent French father during his formative years. Already having taken exception to the man's vocabulary, he now took umbrage. *"Il y a une jeune femme!"*

The Frenchman spread his hands apologetically. *"Ça va très bien, monsieur. Elle ne parle pas français."*

Elizabeth spoke French very well. She opened her mouth to contradict him, then closed it again. Life might be far more interesting—and informative— if these men did not know she understood what they said.

The hope of terra firma beneath his feet spurred Robert to try anything to reach that goal, and he organized his ineffectual crew. By dint of having all three of them hanging over one side as far as they could and paddling with their hands as Armand had done, they managed to turn the boat after a great deal of difficulty, but the sail still flapped. How to go forward against the wind?

Elizabeth, still experimenting with the boom, accidentally filled the sail with the cross wind and sent the boat scooting sideways. From the disaster of his long ago sail on the Thames, Robert remembered that a zigzag course was involved, and more experimenting led to progress. Slowly they began to make headway, but it was nearly dark before they arrived at Armand's Island of the Fox.

Another boat lay at anchor near the shore.

"*Sacrebleu,* it is the ship of Gérard!" exclaimed Armand. "*Les chiens* await us."

CHAPTER THREE

THE ÎLE DE RENARD, an irregular tree-covered hill, rose from the sea at the outer limits of the Bay of Boisvert. Indeed, thought Elizabeth, it looked to be in the shape of a crouching animal, though how it came to be known as a fox seemed to be a matter of wishful thinking on someone's part.

In the gathering dusk, they could still make out the pale hull of the other boat, drawn up to shore in a tiny bay. Elizabeth touched Robert's arm.

"Will they not see us coming?" She found herself whispering, and spoke louder than she had intended. "What shall we do?"

Robert shrugged. "It is no matter. They cannot know Armand is aboard. We have only to be pleasure seekers, planning to picnic."

"In the dark? We must hide Armand, for they mean to kill him; but how? This is an open boat!"

"I shall lie in the bottom," offered Armand. "And *mademoiselle* will cover me with her so great cloak."

"You cannot lie there forever." Robert sounded impatient. He had been watching the shore, and an odd note crept into his voice. "I do not think we need worry. I am not adept at steering against the wind and our craft has a mind of its own. It is veering north and we may miss the island altogether."

Panic ensued. By shifting the sail from side to side, they had maintained their zigzag course and made progress, but each change took a deal of time before they caught the wind. They were well past the island before they managed to turn the boat. They now headed straight for the ocean side of the narrow, tree-covered arm of land that formed the little bay where the other boat lay at anchor close to the shore. Finally, they ran aground in a cove beyond a steep cliff, shielded from the sight of the villains by the sturdy bit of forest.

They struggled ashore and tied the beached sailboat to a tree. Robert collapsed, hugging the ground.

"The first order," said Elizabeth, "is to build a fire to dry Mr. Greenwood's clothes before he becomes ill."

She and Armand collected dry branches and were readying his tinder-box to set them alight, when Robert looked up and realized what they were about.

"Are you planning to set a signal fire?" he asked. "Perhaps to alert Armand's recent friends to our arrival?"

"Dear God!" exclaimed Elizabeth. "How addle-pated can we be? Give me your wet garments, sir, that I may spread them to dry on these bushes."

It was by now full dark, and nothing could be done until daylight. They huddled together for warmth at the base of a tree, the shivering Robert in the middle, and Elizabeth's cloak spread over them all.

"Heavens, but I am hungry," she murmured after a while.

Armand leaped to his feet and bowed. "I go at once."

"Go? Go where?"

"Where but to steal for you the food of those *scélérats*, Gérard and Dupont. No doubt they have come prepared to make a stay while they search for my treasure."

"No!" Elizabeth cried. "Those men mean to kill you! Do not go near them or we are all dead! You will surely make mice feet of such an undertaking."

Robert raised his pale face. "I'll go."

"You!" she exclaimed.

He replied with dignity. "Madam, I admit you have not seen me at my best."

Remembering his nearly running her down in the street, his rude behaviour on the quay and his lack of seamanship, she was forced to agree. "I sincerely hope I have not," she said.

Indignant, he struggled to his feet and reached for his damp coat. "But give me a minute to regain my land legs, and I am off."

Armand immediately promised to accompany him, and they argued, first in English, then in French as they actually began to lay plans. Elizabeth bristled but held her tongue.

She couldn't follow all their rapid, idiomatic speech, but comprehended enough to learn they meant to leave her behind where she would be safe. Indeed, she thought. And who would take care of those two bunglers?

The moon had risen, its soft light giving Robert and Armand a misplaced confidence. Elizabeth soon realized their plan was entirely too simple. Something was bound to go wrong. One of them, they decided, would make a loud noise, an animal cry or perhaps the breaking of twigs as though a large beast approached. Then, when the two pirates went to investigate, the other would steal their food.

Elizabeth hated to be a marplot, but she perceived a large hole in their design. Suppose the men had remained on the boat and had not come ashore? As if in answer, on the other side of the small island a column of smoke from a camp-fire rose above the trees, the plume clearly visible against the moonlit sky.

"Ah," said Robert, in French. "This will make it easier for us to find them. But conversely, they will be able to see us beneath this moon if we are not careful. The actual stealing of the food will be the most dangerous, therefore I think it best I take that part."

Armand was inclined to disagree. *"Mais non, mon ami!"*

"You are the smaller of us," Robert continued patiently. "You must be the animal. You are less easily seen and can elude them if they give chase, a thing requiring more skill than the purloining of their supplies."

This appealed at once to Armand. "Ah. Then I run back here and lure them away while you do the robbery?"

This would not do. "Do you think to lead them to the lady? No, indeed, you will eventually circle around and rejoin me on the other side of their camp."

"You are right as ever. Let us be on our way."

They started off, after adjuring Elizabeth to stay where she was until they returned.

Miss Elizabeth Garner had her own Achilles' heel, the legacy of an insensitive nursemaid who terrorized a little girl with ghost stories. She was a mature young lady now, intelligent enough to have outgrown her childish fear of wraiths and spectres—but she had never before been left alone in a dark wood full of tiny sounds of movement in the bushes. She knew she was being nonsensical. Her agile mind quickly recognized that fact and brought forth a solution.

She took her bonnet from the hatbox. Naturally, the impetuous men had made no provision for carrying off whatever food they managed to steal. They would need that hatbox. She tied her bonnet securely on her head and ran after them, carrying the empty box.

She had gone some way into the dark forest when she realized she was very alone. She ran faster. Where were Robert and Armand? But as she could smell the smoke of a camp-fire, she knew she had to be near. With that as a guide she could not go wrong.

Nor did she. The evil conspirators were camped on shore less than half a mile from the point where Robert's boat had run aground. Elizabeth crept up silently, under cover of the stand of trees, and hid behind a convenient bush.

Never had she seen two less prepossessing characters, though she admitted to herself she might be prejudiced. One, a large, stocky individual, was munching on a chunk of cheese while waving a broken loaf as he talked. Slow of speech, he was easy to understand. The other, smaller, wiry and dark of features, spoke rapidly with a clipped accent difficult for her to follow.

He had a bottle of wine in one hand, and tipped it high for a long drink. Then, as she watched, he used a villainous knife to saw a slice from a fragrant length of sausage. Elizabeth's mouth watered and she swallowed. Her aching hunger became a sharp pain. She grew dizzy from lack of nutrition, and her thoughts flew suddenly to poor Mr. Greenwood, who not only lacked today's meals but no doubt had lost those of several days previous.

The smaller, dark man did not seem to be concerned with the difficulties before the two of them. "It is a small island, Dupont," he was saying. "There cannot be too many places to conceal a chest of gold and jewels, and we have food for several days."

"We should have kept Armand," the man called Dupont argued. "He would have led us to it. We will never find it, Gérard. Suppose it is buried?"

"Do not be a fool, Dupont. Did you see the little bastard carry aboard a shovel?"

Dupont wiped his mouth on his shirtsleeve, grumbling. "Do you mean, *mon copain,* to keep that bottle all night?" He threw a couple of branches onto the fire.

The violet shadows of dusk had deepened to purple and black. The camp-fire blazed up as it took hold of the new fuel. The light reached to Elizabeth's shrubbery. Up to then, the men had failed to notice the wreath of roses creeping up to their camp, but now Elizabeth risked raising her head to peek over her bush just as Gérard happened to look her way.

"There are flowers over there," he remarked, hacking off another slice of sausage. "Demme if they don't look like roses in the dark."

Dupont, his mouth full of cheese, merely grunted.

Elizabeth, rigid with fear, held her breath, willing herself to become a bush.

Gérard shrugged and bit into his sausage, losing interest in roses.

But he might look back at any moment. She dared not move, praying her face was hidden by the leaves.

She had the most horrid thought. Suppose the confounded man decided to pick one of her roses?

She could not run away—he would be sure to notice the flowers were missing—she could not even change her position, though sharp twigs were digging into her back. She was quite immobilized. Oh, why had she worn that hat?

ROBERT AND ARMAND, meanwhile, had made their stealthy way to the other side of the camp. They halted a short distance back under the trees to hold a council of war. Robert, the taller, could see over the shrubbery that edged the woods along the beach. "Two men, all right," he whispered to Armand. "And they have food. There is a wicker hamper between them, and one of them has taken out a large sausage."

"Sausage..." Armand moaned. "Can we not liberate it from those *canaille?*"

Robert shivered in his damp coat. "I'd far rather take back their fire."

"I would see this sausage," said Armand. "These bushes are too high."

"Not high enough." Robert yanked him back. "Quiet! They will hear you."

Armand pulled away. "Only one look." He obligingly spoke under his breath. "I have but to climb this tree."

Before Robert could grab him again, he had swung himself up onto a low branch and begun to work his way towards the tip. It was a small branch. With a splintering crash, he hit the ground.

Robert seized him and dragged him under a thick bush, a hand clamped over his mouth. "Quiet, for God's sake! Lie still! We cannot run or they will hear us."

The men had certainly heard the crash.

"What was that?" yelled Dupont.

"Just an animal," Gérard soothed. "We are alone on this island."

Dupont rose, setting down the wine bottle. He walked to the edge of the circle of light from the fire and peered nervously into the darkness.

"Gérard, it must have been a very *large* animal."

His companion shrugged, but when he spoke, he sounded more than a trifle shaken. "We are safe by the fire, Dupont. Wild beasts fear the flames." He got to his feet, staring about. "Let us find more wood quickly, for we must keep it going all night."

Stepping carefully and each clutching a burning branch for a torch, they left the pool of light made by the fire to forage nearby for dead wood. They passed so close to the bush under which Robert and Armand lay that they might have trod on their fingers had the digits not been curled so tightly. Only the fact that Dupont held his burning brand high, expecting to be pounced on from above, prevented his seeing them.

As Dupont passed, Armand moved convulsively, causing Robert to shove his face into the ground. He spluttered and wriggled. Fortunately, Dupont's large feet stumbling through the undergrowth covered the sounds.

"What the devil are you doing?" Robert demanded *sotto voce* when the big man had gone by.

"A species of beetle," Armand whispered, trying to scrabble away. "I have a terror of the creatures dropping down my neck!"

"You'll be squashed like one if you do not keep still!" Robert suspected he had a few beetles of his own crawling under his coat and across his bare back. He had borne them stoically and it annoyed him that Armand got to complain.

They could hear the wood gatherers making their way back through the trees. It was time to leave. All chance of stealing that hamper was lost, for Dupont and Gérard would remain awake until daybreak, stoking their fire to keep their beast at bay.

WHILE GÉRARD AND DUPONT hunted wood, Elizabeth saw her chance. Abandoning her pose as a rosebush, she tiptoed up to the large wicker hamper and looked in. By the light of the camp-fire, she saw bottles of wine, long loaves of bread, several rounds of cheese—and the remains of the sausage. She licked her lips.

Should she take the whole hamper? But it was far too bulky and much too heavy for her to carry. And if she did drag it away, surely the bad men would know they were not alone on the island. She was thankful she had brought her hatbox, and made a careful selection of items she hoped might not be missed. Into the box went two of the loaves, a flat round of cheese and three bottles of wine.

She looked longingly at the sausage, but dared not take it all. Its absence would be too obvious. She could find nothing with which to cut off a piece. That awful man had carried away his knife, probably in lieu of a better weapon in case he had to slay the beast. Armand. That crash could only have been him. Robert would be out there, as well. She offered up a brief prayer for their safety and took to her heels, far more afraid of live villains than of nebulous ghosts.

Now, if only those men did not miss the rose-bush...

By keeping the rising moon always at her back, Elizabeth found her way back to the cove where their boat still lay aground. She was unpacking her hatbox by moonlight when Robert and Armand returned, empty-handed.

Robert stopped dead, staring at her loot. "What the devil?" he exclaimed.

After one look at his stricken face, Elizabeth knew exactly what to say. "You two were wonderful!" she gushed, managing to sound truly sincere. "Such an inspired diversionary tactic! However did you know I was there?"

"We—" began Armand.

"Be still," advised Robert, hunkering down beside the hatbox. "Let us quit while we are ahead." He gave Elizabeth a sheepish grin and received an innocent smile in return.

Armand peered into the box. "You did not get the sausage!" he complained.

"There was only the one," Elizabeth explained, defensive. "I was afraid they would notice it was gone."

Robert tore one of the loaves into three chunks, broke the flat cheese into pieces over a sharp projection of rock near the water and opened one of the bottles of wine.

"We'd best save the rest for tomorrow," he explained to Elizabeth. "I'll not risk having you go back there."

"Nor would I go again," she declared. "I had quite enough of pretending to be a rosebush."

She regaled them with her experience as they chewed on the tough bread and cheese, washing it down with the wine, the bottle passing from hand to hand. In turn, Armand gave a colourful version of his tree climbing. Elizabeth laughed, and Robert really looked at her for the first time. She was quite well-to-pass there in the moonlight, even after all they had gone through. His admiration for her grew. A most intrepid young lady. Any other he had known would have swooned away in a fit of the vapours long before now.

He shifted his weight uncomfortably, unable to imagine a worse situation in which to have made the acquaintance of so delightful a young lady. He must have appeared a complete fool there on the boat. Seasick! And letting those men rob her at gunpoint without lifting a hand to prevent it. He might not have been able to do much, but at least he could have saved face by trying. He felt himself grow hot at the memory. How utterly degrading a weakness! What must she think of him? And he knew suddenly the answer was of vital importance.

He wanted to know all about her. "How came you into this deuce of a hobble?" he asked. "You must have had a desperate need to reach France to travel alone and take passage on other than the packet."

She smiled. "I thought I had." She told them of receiving a letter from Andrew proposing marriage. "He could only be in Calais this one day.

There was no time for me to write a reply. He said
he would meet the packet, and if I did not come he
would know my answer and go on to Vienna without me." She shook her head ruefully. "It was sheer
foolishness. I could not decide to commit myself to
a life with Andrew until it was too late. Of course I
missed the packet and had to hire what transportation I could."

She bit delicately into a large chunk of the cheese
before going on. "My abigail and my trunks may
even now be in Calais awaiting me, but not Andrew. He will be on his way to Vienna without me,
although I trust he booked passage for poor Mayhew to return to England before he left. Somehow," she added, "I am not devastated. In a way I
am rather relieved to have so great a decision made
for me. I have a suspicion it was the fact that General Lord Cathcart preferred stable married men on
his staff that brought Andrew up to scratch, not my
pretty face."

"It certainly wasn't your taste in headgear,"
Robert teased, suddenly feeling more cheerful.

Elizabeth remembered she still wore her atrocious bonnet, and hastily returned it to the safety of
the hatbox.

"I must suppose," Robert continued, surprising
himself with a twinge of what might almost be

jealousy, "that your Andrew is partial to red roses the size of cabbages."

She took this sally in unexpectedly good part. "And what about yourself?" she parried. "My haste was naught compared to yours. And to brave such a journey in your condition! You must indeed have a powerful incentive!"

He acknowledged a hit with a fencer's *"Touché. Believe me, had I known the severity of the consequences, I'd still be in England."* Turning to Armand, he cleared his throat apologetically. "I think, my friend, I had best tell you who I am." He told him of Mr. Breckenridge's letter, his new title and his decision to go to France.

To his amazement, Armand leapt up and seized him, not to strangle him as he first feared, but to hug and kiss him fervently on both cheeks.

"Mon cousin!" the Frenchman cried. "Old Étienne cannot be happier than I!"

"Yes, well." Robert tried not to scrub at his face and almost succeeded. "I thought you would not like it."

"But it is greatly to my good that you, and not Étienne, are the new *comte!*"

Elizabeth had been gazing at Robert, wide-eyed. "I had no idea I travelled with the nobility!"

He glanced at her and shrugged. "As a title, it is not much, under Napoleon. It is the estate that brought me, for my man of business tells me it is time I settled down, and the requirements of the will include living in the Château de Boisvert for six months and marrying this female—I have her name here somewhere—" He reached into his damp coat pocket for a bundle of papers, tightly wrapped in oiled cloth.

"Delphine," supplied Armand, who had been listening with avid attention. "My Delphine. So it is you who will take from me my betrothed."

"Oh, the devil!" exclaimed Robert. "I had no idea."

"But no, it is not your fault or your doing. The old *comte* would never accept me as a *parti* for his great-niece, owing to the irregularity of my birth. That is why I must find whatever treasure is hidden by my late father, for then I shall elope with my Delphine."

Would this release him from the marriage requirement? Robert wondered. Or might it cancel his entire inheritance? He feared it would.

"As far as I am concerned, as the new head of the family," he told Armand, "you could have the girl and welcome, but I must marry her or I understand the estate passes to the next legal heir."

"Ah, old Étienne. There is one who is most pleased to learn you have been found. When it was revealed to us, he was greatly relieved."

"Just who is this Étienne?" Elizabeth asked. "I should think, if he were the heir before, he would be upset and angry to have Robert turn up."

"Ah, he is the cousin of my *grand-père, le comte.* The last male of the family Boisvert until this son of the younger son was located. He and his wife are long past the age of producing children, and to Étienne, the preservation of title and family name means all. If Robert had not been born, the line would be ended. Old Étienne is as proud of his family as his contemporary, my *grand-père,* and feels deeply the guilt of not having a son to carry on the title of Comte du Boisvert. You are to father that heir and continue the ancient and noble line."

Robert reverted to French. "Does he think, then, that my only use is to serve as a stud for his stable?"

Elizabeth, the daughter of a man with racing stock, stifled a giggle and tried to look suitably blank.

Armand was profoundly offended. "It is a position of the greatest honour, my friend."

Robert saw the Frenchman was quite serious; the Boisvert family meant a great deal to him even though he could not claim the name. Guilt was a terrier worrying at Robert's heels. The entire procedure seemed totally unfair. But for the untimely execution of his father, Armand would even now stand in Robert's shoes and be free to wed his Del-phine. Instead, another man would have the title as well as the girl. It was too much. Poor Armand should at least have his treasure, and he vowed to help him find it. "Where on this island are we to search?" he asked.

Armand brightened at once. "Then you will come once more to my aid? I have only the words of my mother. On her dying breath, she exacted the promise of *mon oncle*—her brother—that he would not reveal the clue until the reading of the will. For that reason, I believe it to be the family jewels, hidden during the Terror so that they would not be confiscated by the *bourgeoisie*. It is vital that I reach my fortune before Gérard and Dupont spirit it away."

"Then," said Robert, who saw a way to remain on solid land for yet a while, "since we are here, let us by all means devote ourselves to the hunt. What is your clue?"

"The exact words of my mother are as follows: '*Cherche à l'île où le renard vert s'élève de l'eau. À gauche, toujours à gauche.*'"

Robert carefully translated for Elizabeth. "Look on the island where the green fox rises from the water. To the left, always to the left."

"Who ever heard of a green fox?" she asked. "Armand, you cannot have it right."

"*Mais oui!* It must mean this island, which is green with trees and shaped like a crouching fox. It is known as l'Île du Renard. There are four more islands, but they are merely large rocks. They go towards the mainland, and are called Les Lapins— the rabbits the fox chases, you understand."

"What I do not understand is why your father would hide his fortune away out here on an island." She puzzled over the words. "And why always to the left?"

Robert had a suggestion based on similar pronunciation. "These words, were they written down?"

"*Mais non. Mon oncle* memorized her speech."

"In that case, in place of *vert*, green, could your mother not have said *vair*, for variegated fur? Foxes come in several colours. Might she not have meant a real fox?"

"But of course!" Armand exclaimed, delighted. "We have only to find a fox's den near the lake in the centre of the island and find in it my treasure. Since Gérard stole from me the false map I prepared for the untrustworthy Dupont, those pigs will not bother us. They will be digging in the sand on an entirely different part of the island. *Allons!*" he cried. "Let us go."

Not at night in pitch darkness, the other two protested. But they only coaxed him to sleep first by promising they would start off at dawn.

"Mr. Greenwood," Elizabeth pronounced firmly, "needs a night of sleep to fully recover."

Robert had to pose an objection to being coddled, but secretly he knew she was right. A truly remarkable young woman.

After a brief argument about whether to sleep on the beach out in the open or retire to comparative safety, hidden under the trees, they finally settled down a distance back in the woods. They lay on Elizabeth's spread cloak, close together, with the damp Robert in the middle to keep him as warm as they could.

An hour before dawn, they were wakened by a blood-curdling scream.

CHAPTER FOUR

ROBERT SAT bolt upright between Elizabeth and Armand, gasping and shuddering as though with the ague, his forehead dewed with perspiration.

"Sir—Mr. Greenwood!" Elizabeth cried. "Was that you? Are you all right?"

He tried to force a casual laugh. "God, I haven't done that for years. My deepest apologies. An old nightmare returned."

Armand regarded him with awe. "A nightmare *très formidable!*" he murmured.

Too badly shaken to temporize, Robert confessed his terror of the water. "When I was a small child, my parents drowned in a boating accident and I very nearly went down with them. A sailor pulled me unconscious from the sea. I have never been able to rid myself of the horror I knew when the water closed over my head and I could no longer breathe."

He rubbed his face with both hands as though to scrub away the feeling of terror and desolation that still haunted him. "Falling into the sea must have brought it all to the fore once more," he added in a flood of embarrassment. "I am so sorry."

Elizabeth promptly cuddled him in her arms as she would have a frightened child. She looked over his head at Armand. "Those dreadful men of yours must have heard. They will be upon us!"

Armand began to chuckle. "It is my hope that it put into them the fear of *le bon Dieu*. They thought I was an animal most large. No doubt they now cling to each other, quite in fear that the beast they heard last night has come upon them."

Robert scarcely heard him. A beast of his own had come upon him. The beast that lies hidden in every man—the primal urge to take his female.

He held a soft, yielding body, and her warm arms were about him, innocently pressing his head against her breast. As his body responded, chaotic thoughts chased through his mind. What harm would there be in a tender kiss to thank her?

A great deal of harm! His honour would not allow him to take advantage of an unprotected female—the feckless Armand would be of no use to her. For the first time it dawned on him that she was completely in his power. A genuine leveller for a gentleman of honour!

Reluctantly, he released her after only a moment of the embrace that had seemed so natural he had felt no need to apologize. However, when the three of them lay back down, he remained awake, remembering, living over the dizzying sensation of being cradled in her arms.

AT THE FIRST LIGHT of day, after an uneasy night listening for sounds of pursuit, the unlikely trio sat on Elizabeth's cloak eating a breakfast of rapidly drying bread and cheese, washed down with wine. Robert had donned his nearly dry shirt and starchless neckcloth. Though sartorially a disaster, he felt more the thing.

"I am going back to do a bit of spying," he announced. "I think we'd best know what those men are doing."

"*Me*, not you," said Armand. "The turn is mine to be the hero."

Elizabeth started to object, and then realized that the little man needed to assert himself to raise his self-esteem after the debacle last night. She caught Robert's arm and held him back. "Be careful, Armand," she admonished him. "They must not see you."

"I will be the mouse beneath the bush, the beetle upon the tree."

"Just keep off those dry branches," Robert ordered. "One look and come straight back."

Armand saluted. *"Oui, mon capitaine."* He trotted off.

Robert and Elizabeth settled down to wait. Robert, looking at Elizabeth with a new awareness, noticed dark smudges under her eyes and a paleness about her cheeks. Unaccustomed to considering the needs of anyone but himself, he was shocked to find he had become protective of and concerned for this intrepid young woman.

No delicately nurtured female should be expected to endure the horrors of being robbed, cast adrift, pursued by what he could only term pirates and forced to spend a night in the open with two men; yet she bore all with amazing fortitude. A woman in a million!

His millionth woman suddenly held up a hand for silence. Robert had just picked up a chunk of the hard bread and crunched into it. She grabbed his arm and took away the remainder. "Hark! Something is coming—"

It was Armand, pelting through the trees. He joined them, his manner bordering on the hilarious. "They have out my so clever map!" he announced. "I see them argue and begin to walk along the beach, away from their boat. Is that more cheese left there? And bread?"

"Armand, in what direction were they going?" Robert demanded. "Not towards us, I hope."

"*Mais oui,*" he replied, his mouth full. "They follow my map. Did I not say so?"

"Do stop chewing and listen," Elizabeth ordered. "I think I hear voices."

Indeed, the low rumble of a man's voice sounded from the farther end of their cove. Then the accusing higher tones of the man called Gérard came clearly.

"Glutton!" he exclaimed. "Do not think I cannot guess you are the one to blame. A dozen bottles of the good red Boisvert we have at the start and now only six! And a round of the best cheese and two loaves!"

"*Sapristi!*" hissed Armand. "They come."

Dupont rumbled in self-defence, but the group under the trees did not wait to hear the outcome. Elizabeth gathered up her cloak without shaking it free of twigs and sand, while Armand and Robert dumped the rest of the food into her hatbox, on top of her precious bonnet.

"That's done it," Robert panted as they ran back into the woods. "They will see the boat and know we are here."

"Oh, and when they see the *bateau,* they will know Armand is here, as well. And they meant to kill him!" Elizabeth exclaimed.

The Frenchman nodded briefly. "That thought has come to me also." He led them at a brisk pace up the lower slope of the hill that formed the island.

Under the concealing green of the trees, a carpet of fallen leaves and moss silenced their footsteps. They might yet get away. Elizabeth drew a hopeful breath as she hurried after the men.

"They will know only that you have been rescued," she said.

"Au contraire." Armand for once was serious. "They will believe I have been picked up by ones who have forced me to disclose the secret of my treasure and are even now being led to the spot. Let us hope they will not kill us all."

"Oh, dear." Elizabeth caught up a dragging end of her cloak. "Suppose they set our boat loose and maroon us on this island forever?"

Like Adam and Eve? The idea appealed fleetingly to Robert, but the presence of Armand dashed his flicker of fantasy, and he sighed ruefully for a hopeless dream.

They came to a stream, rippling and bubbling over a rocky bottom, the rising sun glittering on flecks of foam. Armand turned to follow it up the hill as it cascaded past them in a series of tiny waterfalls. At any other time, Robert thought, a young lady would have been enchanted by this romantic scene, but the terrain had become steep and Elizabeth's feet probably hurt—for his certainly did. Soggy Hessians were not made for mountain climbing. This was not the time for romance.

Of necessity, they slowed their pace. Robert remembered that Elizabeth was carrying the cloak and no doubt the hatbox containing their lunch, as well. He was about to offer to carry it for her when he discovered, to his annoyance, that the over-gallant Frenchman was already doing so, as well as guiding her feet along the easiest path through the trees, holding her elbow in his other hand.

Naturally, he turned on Armand. "Of all the coves on this island, what the devil brought them to ours?"

He had picked the right scapegoat. Armand's face creased in an apologetic smile. "That place is the favourite of the Boisvert family. To picnic on boating trips each summer, you understand. On my false map for Dupont, it seemed the best spot to place the X to mark my treasure."

Robert's mouth had a grim set. "They'll find treasure all right, if they catch up with us. Here, give me that to carry." He snatched the hatbox from Armand, only to see him gallantly relieve Elizabeth of the clumsy bundle of her cloak. "I'll take that, also!"

Elizabeth's smile barely fell short of being coy. "No, really, I can manage quite well, Mr.—my lord."

His temper slipped. "For God's sake! Call me Robert, both of you. After all this, surely we are on first-name terms."

"And I am Elizabeth . . . Robert." She gave him a genuine smile, and for a few moments, he forgot his damp boots and sore feet.

AS THEY CLAMBERED up the tree-covered hillside, Elizabeth watched Robert covertly. She had been all too conscious last night of the bare, muscled chest and broad shoulders she had pressed against her, waiting for his shaking to subside.

Whatever would Andrew have thought! And how nice that she no longer had to worry about the prosy man; he would have been well on his way to Vienna by now, perhaps as grateful as she that he travelled alone. She could not imagine whatever had possessed her to consider marriage to that stiff diplomat with his punctilious manners and prudish mind. If only he could see her now, dirty, dishevelled, tramping along beside not one but two men with whom she had just spent the night! How thankful he would be that she had failed to join him at Calais!

Armand trotted at her side, ever eager to please, but it was Robert who drew her, a moth to the flame she had glimpsed before he had so quickly pulled away from her arms. She had felt his gaze upon her this morning as they ate. Did he, too, feel the powerful magnetism? Alas, he was on his way to marry poor Armand's Delphine and raise sons for the Boisverts. She ordered all thoughts of him away, yet her contrary eyes kept straying to the stiff back ahead of her.

The ground continued to rise beneath their feet until they at last reached the summit of the small mountain that was the whole of the Île du Renard. A turquoise lake nestled before them in a bowl-shaped valley. Hot and tired, they slid down a deep bank and collapsed in the shade of the grove that lined the shore.

Here before them lay a scene as romantic as any young lady could wish for. The fog of yesterday had melted away, leaving a sky of the deepest blue. Fluffs of cotton-wool cloud floated across it, reflected in the cool water below. Feathery green pine ringed the lake, growing nearly to the rim, and occasional rocks broke the surface, tips of underwater hills. A gentle breeze ruffled the water, sending tiny wavelets to the pebbled shore where they lapped and receded with a continuous soft gurgling.

Elizabeth caught her breath and spoke in a hushed tone. "Never have I seen such beauty. I would swear we had stepped from reality, were it not for the birds singing in the trees."

Armand broke the spell, slapping at his forehead. "And the mosquitoes. We are here," he announced cheerfully. "Let us begin our search for the den of the fox."

Robert, however, had seen the deepening lines of fatigue on Elizabeth's face. "Not before we are rested," he decreed. He had contrived to sit close to her, stretching out his tired legs so that one foot touched hers as though by accident. Ever since he had held her in his arms the night before, Robert had become vividly conscious of the feminine attractions of Miss Elizabeth Garner. Her figure, he had already noted, was excellent. She might not be an accredited beauty, her features being pleasant—extremely pleasant—rather than cold and classic, but she held for him a strong appeal far surpassing his admiration for her quick mind and pluck. Luckily, he thought, he was not one to conceive a lasting passion for any female.

What was it about her that attracted him so? Her hair was neither angelically fair nor strikingly dark, but the sun filtering through the trees sparked glints of gold and bronze in her soft brown curls. Natural curls, for the poor girl had neither curling tongs nor mirror. She had nothing, in fact, but the bedraggled gown she wore, her ubiquitous cloak, totally inadequate cloth half-boots and that bonnet. He wondered why she clung to it so tenaciously.

Perhaps because it was her only connection with England here in a foreign land. That must be it. But what a paltry souvenir!

While they rested, they finished the remains of their purloined bread and cheese, passing the last bottle of wine between them.

Armand dusted the crumbs from his stained and dirty breeches and stood up. "Now, *mes amis,* we look for an ancient fox den."

"Why ancient?" Elizabeth asked, shaking bits of bread and cheese from the roses on her bonnet before replacing it in the hatbox. She started to rise. Armand hastily extended a hand to help her up, forestalling Robert, who had not thought of it in time.

"The den must be of many years old," the Frenchman told her. "It cannot be the same fox still living. Though no doubt," he added, brightening, "it will yet be occupied by his descendants."

They walked the perimeter of the lake, peering under rocks and tree roots, travelling always to their left, as Armand insisted.

"Suppose I turn around?" Elizabeth wanted to know. "Then left is the opposite direction. Which would it be?"

He pondered only a moment. "Assuredly, my mother meant facing the lake. Then in our circling, our left is always the same."

Robert made no comment, searching at that moment under a log. An hour had gone by, but no dens had been found save those of a size to shelter ground squirrels.

Elizabeth grew uneasy, having that eerie sensation one gets when one is being watched. She kept looking back over her shoulder. "I think those men have followed us."

"Mais non," said Armand. "Remember my so clever false map. Those villains dig in the sand, thirty paces west from the tree to which we secured our boats, then five more to the north to the line of high tide and six feet down. They are much engaged."

His words did naught to ease her nerves. She still had a prickly feeling.

Robert had become restless, as well. "We get nowhere," he complained. "I do not believe there is a fox on this entire island. It is too small for anything but birds and rodents."

Armand stopped dramatically, struck by a revelation. *"Crac!* I lead you wrong!"

Robert snorted. "That we have gathered."

"I have been blind!" Armand ignored another slighting remark before going on. "It is that the fox is truly green. *Le renard* is our—what do you say—emblem, after the founder of the family, who was known as the Fox of Boisvert because of his clever defence of these lands. There are many images of the fox at the château. Even the escutcheon at the entrance is a copper fox mask—and it has turned green! Every chest, every cupboard, has a latch in the image of our fox, and most are copper and now quite green. It is that each one must be searched."

"Your father could not have hidden much beneath a door knocker or a latch," Elizabeth demurred.

Robert saw quite another side of the matter. "Do you mean we have trudged for miles all the way around this confounded lake for nothing?" he demanded.

"*Non, non,* for it has given me the inspiration. We go now to the château."

But not yet. A large, heavy-set man stepped from the trees before them.

"*Ai!*" said Armand. "It is the pig Dupont!"

This, perhaps, was not a politic greeting. The man snarled and charged at Armand.

Robert leapt to his rescue, striking the big man a wisty castor on the ear. With an animal howl of pleasure, Dupont shifted his attack to this more worthy opponent. Not for nothing had Robert trained for several years at Gentleman Jackson's Saloon. Unfortunately, Dupont had not, nor had he learned the rules of a fair fight elsewhere. He closed at once, hands clawing for Robert's throat until a solid punch caught him in the solar plexus.

With a grunt, Dupont staggered back and Robert dived after him. His feet slipped on the loose pebbles that edged the shore and he fell short. A heavy boot grazed his forehead before he could get up. He caught the leg and pulled. Dupont crashed down, unfortunately on top of him and both men rolled on the ground.

Robert had him in height, but gave away an easy fifty pounds. Dupont got his feet under him and hauled Robert up by his shirtfront. He leaned back to deliver a leveller, only to be rocked by a one-two right and left to his jaw.

Elizabeth danced around the edges of the fray waving a large stick, looking for an opening.

Armand hopped up and down, throwing rocks indiscriminately. He stumbled over a cantaloupe-size stone and heaved it with all his strength. He missed Dupont.

He did, however, catch Robert a glancing blow on the side of the head, dropping him like a felled ox.

CHAPTER FIVE

ELIZABETH SHRIEKED and pushed the surprised Dupont aside. Heart pounding, she crouched beside the unconscious Robert and tried desperately to find a pulse in his wrist.

"You have killed him!" she wailed at Armand, sick with fear. "How could you be so stupid!"

The Frenchman came out of his daze. "I do not understand how this happens," he quavered, stunned. "I aim for Dupont. What goes wrong?"

"He's not dead, thank God." Elizabeth filled her lungs with air as she at last located Robert's pulse. "He is breathing, but why does he not wake?"

As she spoke, another man, smaller than Dupont, and wiry, stepped out from behind the trees. Gérard, the boatman.

He looked down at Robert, who lay sprawled on the pebbled shore, his booted feet intermittently awash in the tiny wavelets.

"My thanks, Armand," Gérard said. "You have saved us much trouble." Reaching for Elizabeth, he jerked her to her feet, twisting an arm behind her back until she cried out.

Armand, who was not without courage, started forward. He stopped in his tracks on seeing the pistol Gérard held to her head. Elizabeth froze as well, feeling the cold, hard muzzle press against her temple.

"No, Armand," she whispered, her throat almost too tight for speech. "Stay back!"

The boatman smiled, a feral sneer. "That is right, Armand. You will do as I say for I believe you care far more for the lady's safety than do I. I will not mind shooting her. She has no place in my plans. You, however, I need alive for a bit more. And perhaps also that one."

He moved the pistol slightly to gesture with it towards Robert, then nodded at Dupont, who had been waiting, uncertain what to do next. "Bring him along."

Dupont scrubbed his bleeding nose on his sleeve. "Why do we not cut the throats of these other two and leave them here?" he demanded. Chilly fingers ran up Elizabeth's spine.

"Fool! We leave no evidence on land when we could throw them in the sea, which cannot be searched. For now we keep them, for we have the lever to make this one talk. You heard him say the treasure is at the château, and he has the clue to its location. We will see how he reacts to the torture of his friends. Pick up the man.''

Dupont shrugged, scrubbed his nose once more and shouldered the unconscious Robert with no regard for his comfort.

''Have a care!'' Armand exclaimed. ''You have there the Comte de Boisvert!''

''Yes, please,'' Elizabeth begged. ''He is badly injured.'' Her voice ended in a squeak of pain as Gérard gave her arm a vicious twist. Her words were in English. The others had spoken in French. She shut her mouth. Now more than ever she should pretend ignorance of the language—it might be their salvation.

Dupont had hesitated, but Gérard motioned him ahead with the pistol. ''Are you then so gullible? M. Étienne is the new *comte*. I have heard it in the village. An old man, not this one so young. Go, and you, Armand, follow. Do not forget I hold the pistol to the head of the woman.''

Hastily scooping up Elizabeth's hatbox and cloak, Armand did as he was ordered.

They climbed the bank, away from the lake, and slipped and slid back down the hillside towards the beach. Elizabeth stumbled and Gérard gave the arm he held behind her another painful jerk. She bit her lip until she tasted blood, but she would not give the man the satisfaction of making her cry out again.

At least he no longer held the pistol against her head.

Dupont walked in front, carrying his burden easily. Robert's arms swung against the man's back, and his head bobbed with Dupont's every stride. Elizabeth nearly wept for him. Oh, if only she had not rescued Armand! Right now, she would have taken pleasure in strangling the bumbling Frenchman.

It took far less time to go down than to climb up, and in less than an hour they were back in the cove where she and the others had gone aground. Why were they there and not at Gérard's boat? she wondered.

"You, Armand," Gérard ordered. "You must return our *bateau*. Loosen it from the other that you may drag it along with us."

"But—" began Armand, horrified.

"Do it," said Gérard. "I leave no sign on this island that may be traced to me." Another thought struck him. "Untie the sailboat, also. Push it out into the water and cast it adrift. If it is found, let whoever discovers it make of it what they wish."

"It is a good boat," grumbled Dupont. "We could sell it."

Gérard snapped at him. "And incriminate ourselves? Better all should believe these fools have fallen from it and drowned."

Elizabeth thought of the schooner in which they had started out and the men who had robbed her and ridiculed her bonnet. Suppose their little sailboat should be returned to them, empty—would they believe themselves murderers? She sincerely hoped they would, for this was all their fault. Conveniently, she blocked out poor Robert's ostentatious display of wealth on the dock in Dover. She even told herself it was partially her fault. She and Robert might have been rescued had she not picked up Armand. But she could not have left him at sea in that little *bateau*. However, it served him right to have to drag it along.

They made slow progress through the trees to Gérard's craft. Armand, who had thrown her cloak and hatbox into the bottom of the tiny rowboat, was sweating and muttering what were without doubt obscene phrases in French as he alternately dragged and pushed the rowboat. Gérard waited for him patiently, seeming to enjoy the panting Frenchman's struggles with the unwieldy *bateau*. But even the oxlike Dupont was beginning to feel the weight of his burden. Robert was not a small man.

Gérard had no such load to carry, Elizabeth thought angrily. She was forced along by his grip on the arm he kept twisted behind her. She tried to kick him in the shins with every step, but he merely laughed. Her half-boots had never completely dried, her ruined stockings had worn holes and blisters had formed on both her feet.

Armand was probably no better off in his damp leather boots. Robert, who had reason to be grateful for being carried, unfortunately was still in no condition to appreciate it.

The mast of Gérard's boat appeared above the trees before they broke through to the shore of the little bay where it was anchored in the shallows. Elizabeth nearly fainted with relief. Her shoulder and arm were one sharp ache, and her head had begun to throb. She longed for her bandbox, lost with the schooner Robert had so foolishly purchased. There were headache powders in her bandbox...and dry stockings...another pair of shoes... She fell to the ground when Gérard let go of her arm. He still held the pistol.

Armand laboured up, dragging the *bateau,* and Dupont dumped Robert's limp body into it. The unconscious man's head hit the wood bottom with a dull thump, and Elizabeth winced. It was a very small rowboat and his long legs dangled over the end.

Dupont dragged it to the water's edge and launched it with a mighty shove. Elizabeth, about to scream in protest, clamped a hand over her mouth as the big man waded in and began pushing the little boat and Robert out towards their ship. He was waist deep when he reached it.

Gérard waved his pistol at Armand and Elizabeth. "Follow him," he commanded.

She was quite willing to go wherever Robert was taken, for she clung to the hope of somehow rescuing him . . . but the water was deep and she was nearly a foot shorter than Dupont.

It was Armand who boggled and hung back. "In that boat? But no."

The pistol stopped weaving and pointed at his chest. "Get aboard."

"I would rather not." He eyed the pistol anxiously, then flapped his arms in an exaggerated shrug and stepped into the water.

Why was he so reluctant? Elizabeth wondered. She had gathered that they were headed for his château, and after all, it was Robert who got seasick.

She took off her half-boots and stuck a foot into the foaming backwash of a receding wave, discovering one reason for Armand's demur. It was freezing cold. She pulled her foot out and immediately felt the pistol between her shoulder-blades. She waded in, holding her footwear above her head.

Armand was now nearly to the boat, and she saw with a flutter of misgiving that the water reached high on his chest. She would be in to her armpits!

The gun prodded her back and she went on. The icy coldness was a growing shock as the incoming waves crept up her body, and the salt stung her open blisters. Slippery pebbles covered the bottom, and she breasted the small waves with care. Suppose she fell! It was not as if she had never swum. She had, of course, but always with an attendant and a bathing machine. She had no faith in Gérard's catching her before she went under and floated away.

As she made her way into the brine, her skirt belled out underwater, rising to the tightness of her high waist. Thank heaven for the heavily weighted hem of her petticoat! She spread out her arms in an effort to maintain her balance, shivering until her teeth chattered from the chill.

Ahead, Armand slipped on the smooth stones and vanished from her sight. He surfaced, spluttering. If only she did not follow his example! Suddenly, Elizabeth giggled uncontrollably. So much for her attempts to dry their clothes! She realized she was giggling, and clamped her chattering teeth together. She was getting hysterical, which would be no help at all. Firmly, she took herself in hand.

She reached the boat, a large fishing smack with a single sail. It was nearly flat bottomed, and redolent of long-expired fish. Dupont stood beside it, setting two large hooks from a hoist above into metal rings on the front and back of the *bateau.* Surely he would not raise the rowboat with Robert in it!

He would. She watched in an agony of anxiety as the huge man climbed a short iron ladder set into the side of the boat and began to crank the hoist. When the dripping rowboat cleared the water, she saw Armand already aboard the fishing boat, reaching out to steer the swinging *bateau* onto the deck. She let out her breath. Robert, temporarily, was safe.

The gun prodded her back again.

"I'm going!" she snapped in English. "There's no need for you to shove."

She threw her half-boots up, and Armand, surprisingly, caught them without losing at least one and dropping it into the water.

Gripping the sides of the iron ladder, she got her feet onto the first of its four rungs. She surged out of the water, drenching Gérard below her as much as she could. Her soaked garments clung to her, outlining every curve. The round iron rungs bit into her sore feet, and she made it up as quickly as she could.

Dupont and Armand were lifting Robert from the rowboat as she clambered over the low rail. She ran at once to his side. The sight of Robert's grey face terrified her. "Is he dead?" she asked Armand, her voice so tight that it squeaked.

"But no, Mademoiselle Elizabeth. He lives. It is I who should die for what I have done to him."

He looked ready to weep. She wanted to say something comforting, but Gérard and his pistol interrupted.

"Over to the cabin wall," he ordered. "Face it. Dupont, tie their hands behind their backs."

Dupont looked about the deck. "What with? I see no loose ropes."

Had Gérard been a female, he'd have stamped his foot instead of using the words he did. Elizabeth knew none of them, but Armand, his brows raised, regarded Gérard and his colourful vocabulary with awe.

"Have you no ingenuity, jackass? Use their neckcloths!"

Armand had kept his garments more or less intact, although they were now well soaked, and he bleated feebly when his cravat was snatched from his neck and ripped into strips. His hands and Elizabeth's were tightly bound. Robert's neckcloth was used to secure his hands and ankles.

There was a hatchway on the stern deck. Dupont opened it so he and Gérard could manhandle Robert's body down into the hold. Elizabeth and Armand were quick marched over to the hatch and ordered to drop down after him. The hold was dark, narrow and too low to stand upright. It smelled overpoweringly of the former occupants, fish whose souls, if they had any, had some time ago answered the final summons.

Elizabeth crouched beside Robert. With relief, she discovered that his breathing, though stertorous, was steady.

Dupont followed them down, creating a crowd. Gérard stayed above, only his head and his pistol showing in the open hatch. The big man had located some ends of rope. "Sit," he commanded Elizabeth.

It was not easy, she found, to sink down gracefully with one's hands tied behind. Dupont pulled her feet from under her, hastening her descent. He then tied her ankles together, but not before she managed to kick him several times.

"*Mais non,* Dupont," Armand objected. "You cannot bind her thus. Suppose we are to sink?"

"Then she will drown," explained Dupont cheerfully. "Come, you are next."

"No!"

"Gérard, you will shoot M. Armand in the leg for me, will you not? Perhaps both legs, since he will not be tied. Then he will not run."

"Certainly," Gérard answered from the hatchway. He made a great play of aiming the pistol at Armand.

Armand sat quickly, thrusting out both feet. "So tie," he said, resigned.

Elizabeth looked at him, and her lip curled. Robert would not have given in so easily. Oh, why had she not found that stone first and clobbered Armand with it?

Finished with his knots, Dupont clambered up the three-step wooden ladder in the bulkhead, and boosted himself through the hatchway. He started to close it, but Gérard stopped him.

"We do not wish to suffocate them," he said. "They may yet be useful." Dupont made some answer, then their voices faded away. The trio in the hold was left alone, sitting on the slotted boards above the bilge, where fetid water sloshed beneath them as the boat rocked.

Robert had begun to moan and stir. Elizabeth called his name, hoping to wake him. "Mr. Greenwood...Robert...can you hear me?"

"Of course I can hear you." He opened one eye and tried to focus on her. "What in heaven's name are you doing here?'' He looked past her. ''Where are we?''

''In the ship of Gérard,'' Armand offered helpfully.

Robert's other eye opened. ''Oh, you are here, as well. I seem,'' he continued uncertainly, ''to have the very devil of a headache. I must have had a cup too many and am jug-bitten. I beg your pardon,'' he apologized to Elizabeth.

''No, no, Robert—Mr. Greenwood. You have been injured.''

At this, he raised his head and tried to clutch his pounding temples, discovering in the process that his hands were tied. ''What the devil?'' he demanded in a weak voice. The floor rocked gently beneath him. He began to feel queasy. He stared around the dark and narrow hold and tried not to breathe in the overwhelming aroma of fish.

''Hell and the devil confound it,'' he muttered. ''Now what has happened?'' He tugged against his bonds.

Elizabeth and Armand both spoke at once.

''An accident, *mon ami*, I assure you.''

''Armand only tried to help.''

Robert laid down his aching head. ''Armand,'' he said, closing his eyes. ''Naturally it would be Armand. Good God, but I have the headache. What did he do to bring us to this pass?''

"It was only my poor aim," Armand hastened to explain. "Instead of the *cochon* Dupont, I seem to have struck you. It was so beautiful a stone," he mourned. "Had it not gone astray, all would now be well."

Elizabeth cut in. "Indeed? Are you not forgetting Gérard and his pistol?"

"I think," Robert said carefully, "you had best give me the tale with no roundaboutation. You, Elizabeth, not that beef-witted cod's head." From above came the rattle of a sail going up the mast and the snap as it filled with wind. "Oh, no," he added. "We are moving. Talk fast."

Shushing Armand, who wished to speak, Elizabeth brought Robert up to date.

He tested his bonds again, the familiar horror gripping his stomach. "I must suppose those men are now taking us out to be thrown to the sharks."

"Not yet," Elizabeth told him. "You and I are to be tortured to make Armand give them the true clue to his treasure."

"Thank you." Robert gave her a twisted smile. "That bit of pleasant news is all that was needed to make this a perfect day."

The nearly flat-bottomed fishing smack, without a steadying heavy load in its hold, rocked and swayed with every puff of wind in its sail. Robert already felt queasy. Confound it! Was he always to be sadly indisposed in Elizabeth's company? Conversation, he hoped, might take his mind from his stomach.

"It's beastly wet in here," he remarked. "And you two appear to have been swimming."

The water in the bilge had reached the floorboards beneath them and sloshed over at every dip and plunge of the boat.

Elizabeth spoke in a tight voice. "Armand, surely the water was not so deep when we were left here."

Armand had been fidgeting unhappily for some time. "I think I had best tell you," he began. "This morning when I went to spy on Gérard and Dupont, they were already quite far from their boat, and how could I let so great a chance go by?"

"What," Robert demanded in an ominous tone, "did you do this time?"

Since Robert could not reach him, Armand explained bravely. "I merely went aboard their boat and crawled down here, where I knocked loose a bilge plug." He saw Robert's expression and went on in a hurry. "I hoped that when the ship was in motion, striking the swells, the plug would soon fall out, which it must have done. I meant to sink *them*, you understand, not us."

"We have once more to thank Armand," Robert remarked sourly. This put them in a devil of a fix. What could they do? "If only my head felt better so I could think." His one overwhelming desire at the moment was to strangle the Frenchman. Luckily, his hands were tied or he might have been hanged for murder—but perhaps that was a better fate than drowning. At the thought of going under all that water, he paled and clenched his fists.

Elizabeth, studying his greenish complexion, became worried. "Perhaps your painful head will keep your mind from your stomach," she suggested hopefully.

He groaned. "You had to mention it."

"My dear sir, you cannot be ill in here!"

"I fear I may have no choice."

The water was now several inches deep and coming in more rapidly. It had risen above the floorboards, and they were getting very wet. Robert's phobia seized him with a vengeance, and he discovered a cure for seasickness—his utter terror of drowning. He felt himself shaking.

A shadow crossed the open hatchway above them. "Hoy!" Robert yelled. By a great effort, he did not scream. "Get us up from here! This boat is sinking!"

Gérard's head appeared in the hatch. He took one horrified look at the water in the bottom and disappeared.

Violent commotion ensued on the deck above, followed by the splash of the *bateau* hitting the water. The sound of oars faded away. Then there was silence, except for the gurgle of incoming water.

"Dear God," Elizabeth whispered. "They have left us here to drown!"

CHAPTER SIX

ROBERT TUGGED at his bonds in a near frenzy, perspiration dotting his brow. "I'd give a monkey for a knife to cut us loose," he muttered.

"I have something less expensive." Elizabeth strained to reach her skirt hem. "If I can but get to the pocket in my petticoat, I may be able to free us. There are scissors in my housewife."

Heavenly words! Robert wriggled over to her. He rolled onto his side, his back toward her, and grasped her skirt in his tied hands. Pushing with both feet and using his shoulder, he managed to scoot upwards across the wet slats and work her skirt nearly up to her high waist—a skill he'd never thought to put to such good use.

"I still cannot reach my pocket," she told him. "It is in front of me and my hands are behind. You will have to find it." She turned over to face his back, and tried to ignore the feel of his hands groping along her thin petticoat until he found the pocket.

He managed to extract the small package containing her sewing materials, but bit back a silent curse when he found it fastened by a button which he could not undo.

"Get it to my hands," she ordered. "I can do it." She rolled over again until they were back to back. As she grasped her housewife, his strong fingers closed on hers and, for a long moment, pressed them between his own.

"Th-thank you," she said quickly. "I have it now." She managed the button with one hand and retrieved her scissors, losing the rest of the contents between the planks of the slotted floor. "Oh, dear, all my needles and threads are gone! Never have I been so disastrously involved with water."

"Never mind that, can you work the scissors?"

She could. Luckily neckcloths were not heavy ropes. After some highly acrobatic manoeuvring, she sawed through one wet thickness enough for him to break free of the rest, only snipping his wrists twice in the process.

He flexed his fingers and sat up cautiously. Surprisingly, his head did not split open as he feared it would. In a few minutes, the bonds on his ankles were off and he tried to stand on his feet in the low hold. Grabbing his head with both hands, he fell to his knees.

"Sorry," he said. "I seem to be a trifle dizzy."

Armand now was stricken by contrition. "Is it that I have broken for you the head, *mon ami?*"

"I thank you for your solicitude," Robert said with deceptive mildness. "I feel no cracks in my skull, for which I am grateful, but if I ever see you again with a rock in your hands, I will use it to spill whatever brain you may have."

Armand nodded, a thing Robert would not have attempted at the moment. "My aim is very bad, *non?*"

Ignoring him, Robert worked Elizabeth's bonds loose and chafed her hands to restore the circulation, a task that seemed to take a long time.

Armand became restless. "I, too, am in need of being released," he reminded Robert.

Conscious of a new intimacy between them, Robert grinned at Elizabeth. "What say we leave him tied as a safeguard for our future?"

"No, no," she returned with a smile that warmed him right through his wet clothing. "We could not be so cruel."

He realized he was holding his breath and let it out in an exaggerated sigh. "*I* could, but I yield to your better nature." He cut Armand loose and returned the little shears to Elizabeth with a courtly bow, a difficult feat in the low hold.

Turning to the Frenchman, he said, "Now is the time for you to make amends. Show me the location of this missing bilge plug."

This Armand could not do. "But, my friend, it is lost somewhere in the bottom of this boat, and I cannot reach between these boards on which we stand."

"The hole," Robert explained patiently. "Where is the water coming in?"

"Ah, it is there." Armand crawled towards the stern and pointed out the spot where the plug had been.

Robert rolled some of the shredded neckcloth into a wad and jammed it in place, managing to stuff enough into the hole to slow the leak. "I doubt this will hold long, but we may be able to reach shore before we sink." He felt Elizabeth's admiring glance and squared his shoulders. "Up you go," he told her, guiding her to the short ladder below the open hatch. His head throbbed, but he didn't care.

Armand crawled up and out onto the deck next. Robert followed him and winced as the sunlight hit his eyes after the gloom of the hold.

"Only see!" Armand cried, pointing behind them. "There go the *cochons.*"

In the distance, nearing the shore of France, they saw the rowboat containing Gérard and Dupont.

Armand frowned. "Unfortunately they have remembered to take the oars. All the same," he added hopefully, "with both in that so small *bateau,* perhaps they will sink."

"Not with the luck we are having," Robert said.

"Mais oui." Armand remained cheerful. "It is that I fear many boards in the bottom of that *bateau* became loosened while I dragged it over the rocks and roots. I regret only that the damage is not severe enough to swamp them too far from shore to swim."

Elizabeth partially forgave him. After all, it was his clever loosening of the bilge plug that had led to Gérard and Dupont's abandoning the ship. "I do hope," she said, "that they both get thoroughly wet."

She looked around and squealed with dismay. Armand had left her hatbox and cloak in the rowboat, and in their haste to depart their sinking ship, the rats had thrown them out on the deck. The box was sadly bent, for Dupont had dumped the unconscious Robert on top of it, so the lid had fallen off. Her precious bonnet had been trampled by large wet boots. The crown would never be the same and the brim was crumpled, but the roses were all there. Elizabeth picked it up and began to check each one, smoothing out the petals.

"You'll never wear that again," Robert advised. "Throw it away."

"Oh, no, never!" She hugged it to her breast. "It—it means a great deal to me."

"Ah, yes. Your Andrew likes it." That could not be a touch of jealousy he felt, could it? He shrugged. "*À chacun son goût.* To each his own," he translated for her in so patronizing a tone that she felt like kicking him.

Which reminded her. "Armand, what did you do with my boots?"

"*Pardon?*"

"I threw them up to you when we first boarded this vessel."

The Frenchman looked around vaguely. "I remember only the so big pistol. I must have dropped them somewhere here."

"We must find them!" Elizabeth exclaimed. "I cannot go about barefooted."

They searched the deck. Robert found one half-boot almost at once, but there was no trace of the other. Armand, feeling his guilt strongly, even crawled back down in the hold to hunt.

"It must have gone overboard," Robert said at last, and Elizabeth looked ready to weep. He reached for her, intending to cuddle her in comforting arms—a most pleasant thought—but she forestalled him by straightening her back and smiling bravely.

"At least I have my bonnet and cloak—and one shoe. I shall survive."

"Let us hope that for all of us," said Armand. "Do you not see where we are?"

Robert and Elizabeth ran to the bow. The boat, still on the tack set by the villains, ran before the wind, perilously close to a rocky shore. They had been carried far beyond the Bay of Boisvert and now sailed along a high cliff with breakers foaming up onto a small beach. Every minute they were coming closer and closer to a number of offshore rocks.

"Damn and blast!" Robert looked at the tangle of ropes, none of which appeared to function like reins. Before he could find the proper one to release the sail, they crashed onto a jagged rock, ripping a hole in the hull.

"Of a certainty," remarked Armand, picking himself up from the deck where he had fallen, "we must sometime learn a better way to stop a sailing ship."

"It works, does it not?" Robert growled. He helped Elizabeth to her bare feet. "Are you all right?"

"Oh, yes. I think so." She looked over the rail anxiously. "Do you think we will stay here? We will surely sink if we drift off."

"We are not far from land. I am afraid we must wade in. It may not be safe to remain with the boat. It might, as you suggest, be washed from the rock and sink."

"It will not be the first time I have been in the water today. My garments are so wet that another dousing will not affect them."

"I will go first," announced Armand. "I will discover the depth."

"Wait." While searching for Elizabeth's shoe, Robert had seen a coil of thick rope in the cabin. He tied one end securely around a sturdy cleat on deck and the other about Armand's waist. "We cannot have you washed away," he explained. "Though I shall no doubt live to regret it."

Armand fingered the rope. "Let us give thanks we were not bound with this."

"It is too big to tie a small knot. I only hope you do not slip out of it."

"I shall cling like death." He clambered over the low rail and dropped into waist-deep water. Robert paid out the rope while Armand floundered some thirty yards to shore. Once on land, he untied himself and pulled in the excess rope, winding it several times around a convenient rock.

"We have now a lifeline," he shouted. "Come along, but hold to it most tightly. The waves are strong where they break."

"I'll go next," said Elizabeth. "I can hook one arm about the rope and hold my hatbox over my head with the other. My cloak is not yet thoroughly soaked. You are taller than I, Robert, and may be able to carry it to shore without further wetting. We may need it again."

Robert had begun to have very warm feelings for the doughty Elizabeth. "We go together," he said, crushing down his own fear. If Armand could do it, then so could he.

He helped her over the side and down the short ladder, handing her the hat box when she had a firm grip on the rope. *It is not deep,* he told himself. *It is not deep.* He climbed down into the water, shuddering as the cold hit him. Every muscle tensed, and the pounding in his aching head blacked out his vision for a moment. But Elizabeth went on, clinging to the rope and holding that ridiculous hatbox over her head. He had to follow—suppose she lost her grip on their lifeline!

Which she did when struck by the first breaking wave.

Robert's terror for himself was lost in his terror for her. He dropped her cloak and his own hold on the rope, seizing her in his arms as the wave swept her off her feet. He carried her past the breaker line, staggering through knee-deep water, which became ankle deep and finally only wet sand.

Elizabeth, still clutching her battered hatbox, struggled in his arms. "My thanks, Robert," she said, "but you may put me down now."

Reluctantly, he set her on her feet. There, for a few minutes, he had felt quite the hero. It was a sensation he had not known since meeting Miss Elizabeth Garner. It did not remain with him long.

Armand, as at home with the sea as one of the gulls that squawked and swooped above them, splashed out and retrieved Elizabeth's cloak. He bore the soggy garment up to her in triumph. "It may be that we need it once more," he said. "It is only to dry it in the sun."

Of which there was not much left, for it rode low on the western horizon. Nevertheless, Armand wrung out as much salt water as he could and spread out the cloak on the sand.

"We should do the same with our clothes," Elizabeth said uncertainly. "But I believe we should first seek shelter. Armand, this is your country. Do you know where we are?"

"We are far north of the château, I am positive. A road follows this coast. It is possible we may secure transport if we meet a coach."

But first they had to arrive at the road. Elizabeth looked up at the cliff in despair. Besides being steep, the ground was rough and rocky.

"I cannot climb that with only one shoe!"

The gallant Armand at once offered to carry her, and she surprised him by succumbing to a fit of the giggles.

"Indeed you could not! Was there ever such a bumble-broth?" she gasped. "What next could befall us?"

Robert had been studying the cliff. "We might drown yet," he told her. "Look at these rocks at the base. Seaweed. I collect there is a high tide in these parts."

"Indeed, yes," said Armand. "When it comes in, these small beaches vanish."

Elizabeth took her remaining half-boot from the hatbox where she had stowed it, and put it on.

"You cannot go like that." Robert picked up her cloak and ripped loose a strip from the hem. "Give me your foot," he ordered.

"What a clever idea!" She held out her bare foot and allowed him to wrap it round and round with the woollen material. "It is not in the height of fashion, perhaps, but it will serve admirably."

Which it did, needing only two stops for rewinding.

The road promised by Armand meandered along the top of the cliff, edging green pasture land fenced with native stone. Elizabeth sank down and leaned against the dry wall, catching her breath while Robert rewrapped her foot.

She looked at her companions and that irrepressible giggle broke through again. "Never have I seen so disreputable a crew as we now appear. We shall be taken for brigands! No carriage will stop for such scarecrows!"

"Ah, you forget." Robert grinned at her. "We are the victims of a shipwreck and must beg indulgence."

Shivering in their wet clothes, they sat by the road, Elizabeth being in no condition to walk.

A long hour passed before they heard the clop of hooves and the creak and rattle of some form of carriage. Dusk and dust combined to hide it from view until it came near. Not a coach, as they had hoped, but a lumbering fourgon, a heavily laden covered baggage wagon drawn by four horses. Robert and Armand waved their arms to stop it. It stopped, but the driver levelled a shotgun at them.

Armand being the only Frenchman, Robert pushed him forward.

Holding his hands high, Armand told their shipwreck story, ending with a plea for transport to the nearest town. He did it very well.

The canny driver lowered his gun and rubbed his chin. "How much," he asked, "will you pay?"

"I regret," Armand replied, "I have no money at this moment, but if you will turn your carriage about and take us to the Château de Boisvert, you will be well recompensed."

The man had by now taken a good look at them. The exact meaning of the phrase with which he answered luckily escaped Elizabeth, but she was sure it was uncomplimentary. Robert found it necessary to grab Armand's coattails to keep him from climbing the coach wheel to draw the man's cork.

During the heated exchange that followed, Elizabeth took a lesson from Robert's action on the quay in England. If the man would not give them passage in his carriage, she must buy it. She stepped behind the horses and was busy for a minute with her scissors and the weighted hem of her petticoat. She returned dribbling several gold coins from one hand to the other.

The driver's eyes bulged, as did those of Robert and Armand.

She stepped to the front. "Suggest this to the man, Armand. Suppose he is attacked by brigands who steal the coach from him? In exchange for gold, of course, to line his own pocket."

Armand repeated Elizabeth's message, and the gun moved to aim at her. She backed up a few steps, treading on Armand's toes.

"Suppose instead, woman, I am attacked by foolish road agents and find it necessary to relieve them of their ill-gotten gains." His eyes, glittering with avarice, lit on Elizabeth. "Hand up those gold pieces or I will take them from your body."

Too late, she remembered that Robert's display had led to equally disastrous results.

That gentleman had had enough of their being pushed about, first by the captain of the schooner, then by Gérard and Dupont and now this. In two quick leaps, he was on the side of the wagon and onto the seat. He planted the startled driver a leveller before the man had a chance to duck. Seizing the shotgun, he tossed it down to Armand and dropped to the ground.

"Enough of this foolishness." Turning to Elizabeth, he snapped, "Had you no more sense than to show gold to that man?"

Elizabeth opened her mouth, and diplomatically shut it again. This was no time to discuss the blackness of pots and kettles.

Armand held the gun pointed at the driver of the fourgon, but Robert took over the negotiations.

"We need transport. Either you will carry us or you may remain here and we shall drive ourselves."

The man worked his damaged jaw experimentally and decided he was able to speak. "For the sum offered by the young lady, *monsieur,* I will vanish from the earth. It is not, after all, my own carriage." He climbed down from his seat.

"Then you'd best remain," Robert told him practically, "and explain to the owner in all innocence that you were robbed. Can we not give you a ride to the nearest town before we steal your conveyance?"

Here Elizabeth voiced an objection. The fourgon was loaded with those furnishings held indispensable for a wealthy female traveller.

"We cannot take another's property," she declared. "We must unload all the baggage."

"Why?" asked Armand. "Here we have bedding, down pillows, clean sheets. And only see the trunks! There will be clothing."

"You could do with a new gown," Robert agreed. "And we could certainly use some blankets if we are to be on the road tonight."

"No, indeed!" Elizabeth was shocked. "The carriage is one thing—we do need it and I will pay for it—but I will not be a thief."

Robert looked at her in some wonderment. Female logic was incredible. However, he gestured to Armand to help him unload the fourgon.

"I cannot. I must hold the gun."

Robert's throbbing temple somewhat impaired his temper. He snatched the gun from him and threw it up into the wagon. The Frenchman took one look at his face, hastily grabbed an armful of bedding, and dumped it out on the road.

The driver was busily secreting Elizabeth's coins on various parts of his person. "There is a carriage following me," he told them, winking at the men. "It is carrying the housemaids and should be right behind." He sat down on one of the trunks and watched them labour. "I shall remain here as you suggest and enjoy a far more pleasant journey." The unloading suddenly went far more quickly and carelessly, and he clucked his tongue in disapproval. They ignored him.

Armand had been eyeing the team hitched to the fourgon doubtfully. "I know the way to the château from here, but I confess I have never driven more than a pair."

Robert had. "I do not have with me my proper Four-in-Hand-Club apparel, but I do not believe these French horses will notice." He threw down the last hamper, to the clatter of shattering china dinnerware. "My apologies."

The driver waved dismissively. "I was not to eat from it."

"Get in," Robert ordered his party, this time beating Armand to the task of assisting Elizabeth. He settled her on the seat, between Armand and himself. "Now where?" he asked the Frenchman.

"Back the way from which this conveyance came."

"Naturally." Turning the carriage, Robert started it down the road.

"We will come before long to the Bois Vert," Armand informed Elizabeth. "The green forest that gave our château—and our family—its name. There is a lane through the trees that will shorten our journey by nearly five kilometres. We have then only twenty to go."

"You will have to point out the way."

"There is an *auberge,* an inn, and then the opening between the trees."

"An inn!" Elizabeth exclaimed happily. "There will be food. And perhaps rooms for tonight—with real beds."

"No, I regret. The Coq Violet is not a place for a lady. Me, I will stop there, and if you have another of those so pretty coins, there is a boy with a horse. He can be sent to gallop ahead to the home of Étienne and advise him of our good health and of the perfidy of Dupont, who is in his employ.

Also there I may procure a sausage and wine for supper, for we will not reach the château tonight.''

"Bread," said Elizabeth. "And cheese if we cannot purchase a meal.'' She had a sudden thought. "Robert, do remember the coach that was following this fourgon. As we have turned around, we will meet it soon. We may be recognized, for the night is not yet completely dark.''

In a very short time, the lights of the roadside tavern came into view, and a travelling coach, no doubt carrying the maids mentioned by the driver of the fourgon, pulled out of the stable yard and came towards them.

"Our friend spoke the truth," said Robert. "Hold on." He sprang the horses and passed the carriage at a gallop, trusting the failing light to protect them.

Somewhat to Elizabeth's surprise, Armand being one of their party, they met with no calamity. The travelling coach continued placidly on its way.

Robert reined in the horses and stopped beneath the sign of the Coq Violet. Elizabeth snipped free another coin and Armand went in alone, Robert not wishing to leave Elizabeth by herself in the fourgon.

Armand returned after a lengthy period, with a round loaf, a bottle of wine and a glum face.

"What now?" asked Robert, resigned. "Could you not send your message?"

"Oh, yes." He passed the bread and wine up to Elizabeth and climbed onto the seat. "The boy is even now on his way. But of sausage, there is none. The young thief wanted the entire coin, and it was only with the greatest difficulty that I also obtained our meagre supper."

A long drive lay ahead of them, and there was no way to procure a change of horses, so Robert slowed to a sedate pace more suited to his pounding headache.

Elizabeth, no longer jolted about, dozed beside him, her head on his shoulder. He longed to put an arm round her, but the four horses, unused to his touch, required both his hands.

Sometime later she roused, sensing a change in direction. They had left the main road and now followed a narrow lane, barely wide enough for the carriage, that led into a dark and thick forest.

"Where are we going?" she asked, casting a nervous glance about.

"Be assured that all proceeds," Armand told her. "We have but entered the Bois Vert."

Elizabeth shuddered. "I don't like it. It has an eerie feel."

"It is lovely in the day," Armand assured her, but that was no help at night. The lane was rutted, the fourgon had no springs and tree branches scraped the roof.

"We shall have to stop," Robert decreed at last, "and wait for dawn before we are hopelessly lost. I can no longer distinguish our path from wide places between the trees."

He steered the fourgon into one of the clearings. "We had best sleep inside the carriage. No telling what sort of animals abound in this gloomy forest." Elizabeth suspected he was only teasing to lighten the atmosphere, but she couldn't help half taking him seriously.

She turned her attention to the bed of the fourgon and became very busy. "Now why," she asked, "could I not have included the bedding in our purchase of this vehicle? We cannot lie beneath my wet cloak or we shall all develop an inflammation of the lungs. Perhaps it will dry overnight." She spread it over the seat outside.

Robert watched her, trying to smile in spite of the head-splitting pain that throbbed steadily. "We shall have to cuddle to keep warm," he said, and realized that would be the only reason. Heretofore, any young miss who allowed herself to be caught in the night with one of his ilk would be considered fair game. Why did he hold back from this one? Then it hit him. She *trusted* him. He had never before been trusted by a female in any situation, let alone in the dark. He perceived an insight to his character that startled him.

It was in a thoughtful mood that he helped Armand unhitch the team. They had found a good spot to camp, for there was a stream nearby and grass underfoot. They took the horses, one at a time, to the water, and Armand tethered them by their long reins at a spot where they could graze.

They lay down in the fourgon necessarily close together, for the bed was barely wide enough for three. The night passed slowly for Elizabeth, who heard animal noises on all sides. She knew it could only be the horses moving about as they searched for grass, but nevertheless, she was deeply thankful for the shelter of the fourgon and the company of two men and a shotgun.

No animal sounds wakened her in the dark, cloudy morning. With good reason. All four horses were gone.

CHAPTER SEVEN

ARMAND WAS abjectly apologetic. "Never," he explained with chagrin, "have I been good at tying the knots. It is possible, however," he added hopefully, "that our horses have not gone any great distance."

"Indeed." Robert glared at him. "It is far more likely that they have gone home."

"Home!" Elizabeth had climbed down from the fourgon and joined them. "Where could they possibly live?"

"They were quite fresh when we, ah, acquired them, no doubt changed at the last posting inn. Once unrestrained, a working animal most frequently heads for the stable where the hay and oats are laid on. It's my guess they are miles from here by now."

"There is a posting inn some ten kilometres south of the Coq Violet," Armand put in helpfully. "No doubt we shall find them there."

"That we shall not. It would be stupid as well as nigh on impossible to make our way such a distance."

Elizabeth glanced from one to the other. They squared off like two squabbling little boys. "May I suggest we face that possibility after we at least try to find them here?" she asked in the most reasonable of tones. "They may merely have wandered along that stream in search of better fodder. There is far less grass here under the trees than I realized in the dark of night."

Robert, taken aback, wondered why she must so often be right. His own fault, he admitted to himself. He was quite unaccustomed in his previous existence to looking before he leapt. It was high time he grew up! "Come along, Armand," he ordered. "Let us retrieve those absconding beasts if they be still here."

He noticed that Elizabeth was tightening the wrappings about her bare foot, preparing to accompany Armand, who had already started off. "What," he asked patiently, "do you think you are going to do?"

She looked up in surprise. "Why, help you hunt for our horses."

"Think," he said. "You cannot hop about in a forest with only one shoe and the other foot ravelling loose every few minutes. You'd be a liability rather than a help.''

She conceded the point, though reluctantly, and he drew a complacent breath. This time it was he in the right.

''Up you go,'' he said, all masterful as he boosted her onto the seat of the fourgon. ''You will stay here while we do the hunting.''

''Alone?'' She glanced about nervously.

He handed her the shotgun. ''Here. Should any lion or bear attack you, you may blow a hole clean through it.''

She took the gun from him gingerly. ''I do not know how to shoot.''

''I'll show you.''

She shrank back, laying the heavy gun on the floor by her feet, and refused his offer. ''No, indeed! Absolutely not!''

''Why not? It is quite simple. Even a female—''

''It is not that,'' she reproached him primly. ''Good heavens, suppose I accidentally shot you or Armand if you appeared too suddenly?''

''Well, Armand...''

''No, no. Do not be nonsensical. I will not take the chance of becoming a murderess, even of Armand. It is far better that I do not understand how this devilish device is worked.''

"Ah, yes. Regretfully, I agree it may be best that you do not know."

She gave him an impish smile that caused him to catch his breath. "You may be sure if anyone—or anything—creeps up on me, I shall merely wave the gun as Armand does, and it will suffice."

With that he had to be satisfied. Having no real fear of her being in any danger, he joined Armand, who was meandering aimlessly among the trees.

For what little comfort it gave him, he, and not Elizabeth, was once more right. They returned empty-handed—if one could use such a phrase in regard to the absence of four stalwart coach horses.

"They are long away," he told her as he came up to the fourgon. "We found hoof prints and torn-up soil where they broke loose and definite signs of a number of horses galloping back along the lane we followed."

Elizabeth frowned. "I see." She turned to Armand. "Are we likely to be rescued? Is this road much frequented?"

The Frenchman shrugged. "As you see. There are not the ruts of carriage wheels in this lane. Owing to the narrowness of the passage, it is most used for the walking or the riding of a horse."

"Then why," Robert demanded, "did you put us on it with this monstrous wagon?"

Armand shrugged again, becoming very Gallic, and extended both hands, palms upward. "But, my friend, we wished to reach the château by the method most quick. As I promised, this is the way of the shorter route...." His voice died as he observed Robert's expression.

"He meant well," Elizabeth soothed. "He...he *always* means well."

With little to eat the day before and no hope of breakfast, Robert found his nerves were frayed about the edges like worn coat cuffs. He controlled his temper in view of Elizabeth's determinedly cheerful stoicism. He quirked an eyebrow at her with a rueful smile, and attempted to lighten the situation. "I fear we must abandon our splendid carriage. We cannot pull it. It requires four horses and we are only three."

She rewarded his effort with that quick amused smile that so besotted him. "I collect the castle clock has struck midnight and we are left with only a few mice and an empty pumpkin."

He tried to return her smile, but the seriousness of their situation sent it awry. "We have no choice but to continue our journey by shank's mare." The affair had come to so dreadful a pass that he was sure it could not get worse.

But now it did. The morning was grey and overcast, a dark sky loomed overhead and the hovering clouds threatened to let go. Their plight was so calamitous that the comic side struck Elizabeth.

"And I wondered what more could befall us!" She looked up at Robert, and the first raindrops spattered on her upturned face. "More water!" The absurdity of their position overcame her, and she succumbed helplessly to giggles.

For a moment, Robert stared at her, then an irrepressible urge to join in her merriment grew within him. Never was there so valiant a woman! He laughed aloud and caught her up in an appreciative hug, kissing her soundly on the cheek.

Armand, who was getting rather wet, circled a forefinger at his temple. "Gaga," he muttered and sought shelter in the fourgon.

All too soon for Robert, Elizabeth removed his arms from about her. "We'd best follow him," she said, and the quaver in her voice matched the shake in his hands as he hastened to help her aboard.

They huddled close together in the covered fourgon, watching the downpour through the open back of the wagon. Too late, Elizabeth remembered her cloak spread over the seat outside. It no longer seemed to matter if it became soaked again. She and Robert exchanged tentative smiles, both conscious of the new camaraderie that surpassed even their growing physical awareness of each other—but not that of their empty stomachs.

Armand shifted uncomfortably. "I do not wish to introduce an unpleasant subject," he said at last, "but I do not believe any part of this vehicle to be edible. We cannot remain stranded here forever."

Elizabeth felt Robert release the hand of which he had somehow gained possession.

"It is your turn to be right," he told the Frenchman. "How far do you think we are from civilization?"

"The village of Boisvert." Armand nodded. "A kilometre more or less this side of the *château*. Possibly a matter of two hours on foot."

Robert sighed and clapped his hands on his knees. "There is nothing for it but to start. We cannot become much wetter than we already are. It seems, my poor Elizabeth, that you must walk after all on your uneven feet."

She smiled far more bravely than she felt. "I shall survive."

"Good girl." After checking the wrappings on her foot, he swung lightly to the ground, splashing as he landed, and held up his arms to help Elizabeth.

She was quite ready to leave. The rain had already settled into a gentle drizzle and the interior of the elderly fourgon had become stuffy in the humidity, redolent of mildew and age. Outside, she breathed in the rich scent of wet earth, spiced with pungent odours from the varied trees and damp undergrowth. Overhead, the lowering sky, heavy with deep grey clouds, created a dark and gloomy tunnel of the lane through the trees. The rain might have ceased, but the remaining dank mizzle had the feel of lasting for eternity. She gathered her sodden cloak about her. ''I suspect we are in for a continuance of this heavy dew.''

Robert had kept a casual arm about her shoulders when he set her on the ground and he now gave her a rallying squeeze before releasing his hold. ''A bit of mist will not deter us. After what we have been through, this is comparatively dry.''

She smiled. ''At least we cannot become any wetter. I for one have reached the point of saturation.''

''It is good for the crops,'' Armand offered. ''This we are in is timberland of the best.'' He began to name the trees, but she held her hands to her ears.

''Please, Armand, not now!'' To city-bred Elizabeth, one tree was much like another, and she preferred it that way. She could see these that surrounded them bore leaves of various shapes, but at the moment she had no desire to add to her knowledge.

With the cessation of the downpour, the tumbling music of the stream redoubled. It held little charm for Elizabeth as they began to walk along its bank, nor did she appreciate the gentle pitter-patter of raindrops dripping down the back of her neck from the anonymous trees. She pulled the wet hood of her shortened cloak over her head. It gave no protection at all, but then Robert and Armand were bareheaded and their coats were soaked through.

Armand in particular, with his Continental longer hair, resembled the proverbial drowned rat. She stole a glance at Robert, striding beside her, godlike in his sovereign disregard for the elements. His hair had tightened into ringlet curls, more perfect than any valet could produce. If only that valet were here to shave the stubble from his determined chin... Musing, she stepped into a puddle with her wool-wrapped foot, and the cold water seeping up to her ankle brought her down to earth. Truly, she had had enough of this.

As they walked along, the men conversed in French so as not to worry her, secure in their belief that she did not understand. They succeeded only in adding to her discomfort, for they seemed concerned for her ability to keep up. She grew *more* concerned as she sensed their underlying uneasiness for her safety. All at once, the forest, as well as being rather too moist, became a dark and dangerous place. Wild beasts? Or wilder people? She felt a prickling up her spine as though they were being followed.

"Armand," she interrupted them, "are there brigands in these woods?"

"Of a certainty," he assured her. "Such types abound in this vicinity, I promise you."

Robert carried the shotgun. She clutched her hatbox in one arm and clung to his coat sleeve with the other. Smiling down at her, he pulled his sleeve away in order to put the arm around her instead.

He squared his shoulders and expanded his manly chest, feeling very protective. It was most satisfying to reverse their roles to what they should have been. For almost the first time since leaving England, he began to feel like the out-and-outer he knew himself to be. A winner in all he attempted at home in England, he felt he had not handled himself well at the beginning of this adventure. But of late! He had disarmed a man holding a shotgun and proven his skill at driving a four-in-hand, managing the fourgon with ease. While he'd had a team, of course. Now if only he could solve their current dilemma...

Miraculously, the solution was granted him. A single horseman, wearing an ancient frieze coat and with a scarf tied over his lower face, rode into the track before them. He yanked a dilapidated straw

hat down over his eyes and dramatically bran-
dished a pistol.

"Hold!" he cried in a quavering voice.

Elizabeth squealed. Here was the brigand promised by Armand!

This was just the action Robert had been long-
ing for. He set Elizabeth gently behind him. Raising the shotgun, he aimed it at the startled road
agent.

"Need I point out," he said, hoping all at once
the man had but one pistol, "there are two of us
and only one of you. Shoot me," he went on, "and
this stalwart by my side—Armand," he explained
in English to Elizabeth, "not you—will take this
gun and blast your head off before you can re-
load."

"Even sooner," agreed Armand, delighted with
this turn of events.

"We require your horse," Robert told the brig-
and happily, feeling rather above himself. "I have
no compunction whatever regarding the blowing of
a vast hole through your chest if you do not dis-
mount at once."

The dumbfounded road agent complied.

"Armand, take his pistol from him before
someone—and he knows whom I mean—becomes
a trifle dead." He gestured for Elizabeth, who had

been watching hopefully, to move to the side of the horse.

Their bandit came to life. "Here now! You cannot leave me afoot!"

"We can and we will. You may follow us if you wish and reclaim your mount when we reach the village."

Armand tugged at his sleeve, shaking his head. "Not, I think, to walk behind our backs!"

He had a point. Robert waved the shotgun. "It might be best if you proceed before us."

Armand now held the pistol on the man. His method was clumsy, using both hands, but nonetheless effective.

Elizabeth had a sneaking suspicion that with this second hold-up and seizure of another's property, they had quite changed places with the poor bandit, who appeared completely confused. However, with the prospect of a ride to ease her uneven feet, she did not argue.

Robert put down the shotgun, lifted her up onto the saddle and handed her the battered hatbox.

An accomplished horsewoman, she managed to cling to the animal's mane and sit sideways, thereby preserving her modesty in the narrow skirts that would not allow her to ride astride.

Armand went ahead, herding before him the feckless Robin Hood of Bois Vert, who complained querulously all the way. Robert picked up the gun and proceeded to lead the horse by the reins. Elizabeth carefully refrained from telling him she was quite capable of managing the horse. Well, the combination of the hatbox and a man's saddle did create a slight problem. She submitted meekly to being led.

She rode in reasonable comfort on the surprisingly docile horse, her hatbox on her lap and her eyes on the tall broad-shouldered figure walking by the head of her mount. It must have been Wednesday by now, she mused. If she were home in England, she'd be preparing to attend Almack's evening assembly. Did Mr. Robert Greenwood ever grace its rarefied halls? She might have seen him there and never come to know the man behind the fashionable façade he'd no doubt present to the world of Polite Society.

As though conscious of her regard, he looked up at her and smiled. "Are you all right?"

She nodded. "In far better case than you, I fear. My grateful feet owe you their thanks."

He grinned and turned his eyes back to the rough lane.

He liked her, of that she was sure, but how could he admire her as she now appeared? It had somehow become infinitely important to her that he should someday see her looking her best . . . before he married that French girl and passed from her life.

She thought longingly of the new gown she had bought for Almack's, a most becoming toilette. She had planned to wear it at her own wedding—to Andrew. She suppressed an involuntary shudder at her narrow escape. Would Robert ever see her in such ravishing attire? Where was that gown now? she wondered. Probably still in her trunk, somewhere in France, unless Andrew had sent both her baggage and Mayhew back to England. Better Mayhew than she!

With a startling twinge of surprise, she realized how much she'd rather be here, drenched to the skin, her hair a tumbled bird's nest, and her carefully chosen travelling garb in a condition to send her poor abigail into a near-fatal fit of the vapours. If only this adventure could go on forever and ever and they never need reach that beastly château where Robert meant to marry that loathsome female!

She made a small disgusted sound, and he looked up again. "Tired?" He sounded truly concerned, and she hastened to reassure him.

And reassured he was, for she appeared quite rested. He could see that Elizabeth sat the horse easily—was there nothing she could not do? He drew a breath of relief and straightened his shoulders, feeling quite the dominant male. Had he not procured a horse for her when she needed one? Wonderful woman though she was, she had been close to collapse and surely could have walked no farther in her one boot and wool-wrapped foot.

In his bone-weary state, he felt only an enormous surge of gratitude to have come by that convenient horse so easily.

It did not occur to him to wonder at so opportune a meeting.

CHAPTER EIGHT

THE SUN came out as they emerged from the trees, glistening on an ocean of green, stretching over low, rolling hills. Grapevines marched in serried ranks as far as the eye could see. Armand brought the party to an abrupt halt and waved a hand, the one not holding the pistol.

"You see before you the vineyards of the Château de Boisvert," he told them proudly. "Tended by my family for more than thirty generations."

Elizabeth, properly impressed, gazed in awe. Never had she seen grapes actually growing, let alone in fields that seemed to go on for miles. The sheer beauty of the scene held her spellbound. Beneath the blue sky, the grey clouds sprouted white edges as the sun drove them away. Men in straw hats and bright tunics and women in colourful kerchiefs moved among the carefully tended vines, and the sea of green seemed to bloom. Elizabeth drew in a deep breath, sniffing with pleasure. Even here by the road, far from the wine presses and wooden barrels, the rain-freshened air was flavoured by the scent of spirits.

"Incredible!" she breathed.

Armand flashed her a radiant smile. "Welcome to my home." His glow faded. "To Robert's home—or that of Étienne."

Robert, who had been staring open-mouthed, came to life. "This belongs to the estate? All this?"

The Frenchman nodded. "My distant ancestor seized the château and the surrounding countryside in the eleventh century. He was granted only the title of Comte de Boisvert by the king and earned his name of the Fox by defending his right to the land. It was he who planted the first grapes. The vineyards are the personal property of the Boisvert family, to do with as they wish. Only the title is passed on to his heir. The vines are yours, according to the will of my *grand-père...if* you marry my Delphine."

Feeling a trifle shattered, Robert hoped there was an excellent land manager. His only acquaintance with grapes so far was through the contents of a wineglass. He had never known responsibility, and this visible reminder that his simple life might soon be at an end quite overwhelmed him. The great inheritance he had viewed as a vague treasure house into which he could dip at will, now boded fair to be a millstone about his neck.

Armand prodded their prisoner in the back and steered him into a lane that wound away from the road, between the rows of vines.

"The village lies over this hill," he said. "We will be able to secure a carriage of sorts for our lady and dispense with this *chien* and his plough horse."

"Plough horse!" the brigand exclaimed. "This animal is from the renowned stable of—" He caught himself and stopped.

"Then I suggest you return it to the proper owner," Robert said, disapproval in his tone. "Horse stealing is a serious offence."

The bandit clamped his lips shut behind the concealing scarf and the party continued in silence.

Robert stared about uneasily. Surely an enterprise of this size required a deal of clever management—but think of the income! He would be wealthy beyond his wildest imaginings. His thoughts rambled chaotically. He was sorry for Armand, losing his Delphine as he would...and not a little sorry for himself, tied to a woman he had never seen...just when he was beginning to discover another... A fortune such as this would be hard to resist...but so was his growing *tendre* for Miss Elizabeth Garner....

As THEY CLIMBED to the crest of the first hill, the warming sun raised a gentle steam from their wet garments. Elizabeth struggled unsuccessfully to free herself from her sodden cloak, but between juggling the hatbox and clinging to the horse's mane, she had to give up.

Ahead, the roof of the first building to appear showed over the rise. It turned out to be a barn, solidly built of the native grey stone, with a thatched roof that steamed like Elizabeth's cloak.

"There," said Armand, "we have now the barn of old M. Gautier, who will not mind if we take shelter and make ourselves more presentable."

The time had come, Elizabeth felt, to part company with their hapless brigand before they reached civilization—where the man might turn *them* over to the law for the theft of the horse. She tossed the hatbox to the ground and slid after it before Robert could come to her aid.

He leapt to catch her as she landed. For a minute, he held her in his arms as though loath to let her go, and her heart began an unsteady beat. Really, she had to stop this! Only she felt so safe, so warm...but he was to marry another in such a short time. Their adventure was nearly over. Then why not seize what little she had left? She pressed against his broad, damp chest and felt a quiver run through him. She raised her head and the look in his eyes . . .

"Do I get my horse back now?" the brigand demanded in Robert's ear. "You said when we reached the village." His voice took on an anxious whine. "This is as close as I care to get."

Robert dropped his arms hastily, and Elizabeth stepped back, making an unnecessary fuss over retrieving her hatbox while she regained her composure. Robert picked up the shotgun from the ground, where he had let it fall when he jumped to catch her, and turned it on their captive.

Armand came up, waving the pistol in a reckless manner. "He walked right past me," he complained. "I could not in such a hurry figure how to shoot this contrivance."

Elizabeth straightened up, once more in control of herself. So she was not the only one with no knowledge of such dangerous firearms. For a moment she quite liked Armand.

"Thank goodness you could not manage it," said Robert. "We have not the means of disposing of a body in so public a place." He nodded to the bandit. "Indeed, gallows bird, I suggest you take yourself off."

The man already had the reins and was mounting awkwardly.

"I must thank you for the loan of your horse," Elizabeth told him in English, remembering she should not know French until she could find a convenient moment to explain why she had fooled Robert and Armand.

He replied only with a curt grunt as he gained his seat, and Elizabeth had another thought. "The poor man," she said. "How is one of his occupation to survive without his pistol?"

Robert was beginning to understand her freakish point of view. "You are right," he said solemnly, taking the gun from Armand. After unloading it, he returned the pistol to the dumbfounded brigand.

Elizabeth watched as the man rode off down the hill to the lane, where he turned, not towards the Bois Vert, but in the other direction. "Why," she exclaimed, "he is not going back into the woods!"

"By the way he travels, he will come only to the home of Étienne." Armand shrugged. "Let us proceed to the château, where by now we are expected."

So they were to see the famous château at last—and the residents would soon get a look at them. Elizabeth glanced at her dishevelled companions, and then in dismay, down at herself. One shoe, her cloak soaked and the hem tattered, her once fashionable gown a travesty, stiff with salt and wrinkled. Worse, her hair had to be a disgrace.

"I refuse to be seen," she declared, "until I can at least comb my hair and wash my hands and face."

"And you and I must have a razor." Robert, who had been eyeing the growing beard on the Frenchman's face, rubbed his own darkened chin. "They will think we released the wrong brigand."

Armand, so close to home, was equal to the occasion. "I will fix all. It is only for me to go to the tavern in the village for combs and razors and perhaps more wine." He licked his lips. "And a sausage."

Elizabeth knew a penetrating pang of hunger and saw Robert clamp an arm over his rumbling stomach.

"Must you mention sausage?" he complained. "By all means, you are the one to forage for us."

"Yes, indeed," Elizabeth agreed. "You are in by far the most presentable state." She turned her back and raised her skirt in order to take her tiny shears from her petticoat pocket. Snipping another coin from the weighted hem, she handed it to Armand. "Procure for us some form of transportation, but first bring food and a comb!"

"When we reach the château," Robert told Elizabeth stiffly, "I will repay every penny you have spent. I am wealthy, am I not?" he asked Armand.

"As I assured you, my friend, every grape is yours. Once you marry my Delphine."

"Yes, well..." Robert looked away, uncomfortable. "I do have some blunt of my own, once I can get a letter of credit from England."

Armand pocketed the coin and gave a few ineffectual brushes to his garments, making no impression on the dirt and stains. He shrugged and grinned. "Oh, but Jacques at the *auberge* will take pleasure in the sight of me! Wait here in the barn. I shall not be long. And this time I will not be cheated, for you may be sure I am well-known to the publican."

He strode off towards the cottages nestled in a clearing among the solid expanse of grapevines at the bottom of the hill.

Elizabeth allowed Robert to take the hatbox from her and lead her into the stone barn. A cricket chirping by the door silenced as they approached. She wrinkled her nose at the faintly acrid smell of moulding piles of hay and the dust raised by their feet. Lacy curtains of cobwebs hung from every beam. Apparently the place had once been used to store fodder for the winter. No doubt the heavily thatched roof now stored a vast army of insects. Just so they remained up there!

It was darkish and cool inside the stone building—which was probably full of rats. Elizabeth shuddered and hung back. Robert placed an encouraging arm about her—an act that was becoming a habit with him. Not that she objected.

Nor did he. He had come to value every moment when he could act the hero before this competent young miss. It pleased him immensely to find a soft and vulnerable side to so stout-hearted a lady. He settled her on a stack of fairly clean hay and piled more behind for a backrest. She shivered again, and with a rush of protectiveness, he realized she must be at the point of collapse from hunger and fatigue. As she had comforted him after his nightmare on the island, he cuddled her in his arms.

"Only a little time more," he whispered into her tangled curls.

He knew a deep regret. Only a *very* little time more and he must become a *comte* and marry Armand's Delphine or else reside in France's equivalent of Fleet Street debtors' prison until he could get a letter of credit from England. As his pouch was gone, he could not purchase food or drink or pay his shot at an inn. He'd have to communicate at once with old Breckenridge and explain how he had lost enough gold to last him for a year. Meanwhile, he must beg shelter from this Étienne, who would inherit all.

He sat, gripping Elizabeth tightly in his arms, suddenly feeling sand-bagged.

Confound it, he was thinking as though he had made up his mind to give up all for a woman who probably cared not a jot for him except as a friend and temporary protector. She had seen him in so degrading a light so far.... He'd made no attempt to fix his interest with her, and doubted that he could after this adventure. He could never live down those miserable hours of retching over the side of the boat—and she knew of his cowardice in the water. Devil take it, he'd have to remain in France forever. He *could not* cross that hideous channel again. No course was open for him but to wed the unknown Delphine.

What would Elizabeth do? he wondered. Would she return to England and marry her Andrew, after all? And what would *he* do without her? He had become far too fond of this intrepid young lady. Indeed, the sooner this adventure was resolved, the better for him.

ELIZABETH HAD NOT realized how weary she had become until now that their journey was at an end. Exhausted to the point of no longer caring about decorum, she rested her head on Robert's shoulder, relaxing in his arms with the feeling she had reached a safe haven. He was so strong, so brave. And so chivalrous. Never had he taken advantage of her plight, for one could not count that friendly salute on the cheek in the rainy forest. She admitted to a sneaking regret. At the very least, he could have attempted to kiss her that night on the island...or in the dark fourgon...or now in the gloom of the barn. Was he, too, thinking longingly of what might have been? She raised her head to study the handsome features so close above her.

Truly, he appeared a most dangerous male with his tousled, matted hair, the black stubble on his chin and his hungry dark eyes. A hunger that had nothing to do with Armand's sausage. A tingle raced along her spine. She should be terrified to be alone in his company—in his power!

She looked up just as he chanced to look down at her. Their eyes met, and his lips were inches from hers. So short a distance. He closed it.

His kiss was tentative at first, but then, impulsively, she responded. Her arms went about his neck, pulling his head closer to hers, clinging to him for what might be the last and only time. She devoured him with her every sense, storing up the sensations as the old barn once stored its hay. The strength in his arms...the sound of his soft moan as his lips sought hers again...the taste of salt still on his skin...the fire that glowed in his eyes...even his warm, masculine odour—a scent that must reflect her own after sleeping two nights in all her clothes! She drew back, embarrassed, but his embrace tightened and she no longer cared.

His fingers tangled possessively in her hair, and his lips found hers once more, this time anything but tentative.

After a long minute, he pulled back slowly. "Oh, the devil!" he murmured, his eyes filled with wonder. "I—I beg your pardon. I should not have done that."

When Elizabeth regained the use of her vocal cords, she murmured, "Not...not at all. My fault."

"No, no, all mine."

"Whatever," she conceded. "But it must not happen again." Her arms circled his neck, and it was some time before she could speak. "We cannot," she told him. "Remember your Delphine."

Armand's Delphine, she reminded herself—if only they could locate his green fox. Would that free Robert? She pushed him away.

"We must help Armand find his treasure. Surely if this Delphine elopes with another man, they— whoever *they* may be here in France—cannot expect you to marry her."

Robert shook his head, his expression uncertain. "This Étienne. From Armand's manner, I fear he is one to take advantage of every technicality."

Then he meant to marry that female to gain possession of this great estate! This interlude with her meant nothing to him. As it should not. Whatever had she allowed herself to think, just because he finally did what she had longed for him to do—gave in to an impulse to kiss an available woman. The consequential embrace was her own fault, as she had told him. She had *asked* for it. Well, had she not received what she wanted?

He reached out his arms to hold her again and she suddenly awakened to what might happen if this sort of thing continued here in the barn with so dangerous a man. She bounded to her feet, losing the strip of wool wrapped about the one and tripping over the flapping end. She sprawled face down in the hay, and instantly Robert was bending over her, attempting to help her up.

Armand chose that inopportune moment to arrive. He coughed discreetly from the doorway and they scrambled apart, Elizabeth smoothing down her bedraggled skirts. She felt her face flaming.

"She fell down," Robert explained too hastily.

The Frenchman politely ignored his remark. He came in, bearing a basket from which sprouted a fresh yard-long loaf.

"Only see," he said with pride. "I have had the luck. In the tavern was Gaston, who drives a wagon to convey the grapes to the winery. He will come as soon as he unloads, and transport us to the château." He set the basket on the floor and squatted beside it, passing out the contents with a triumphant air. "The loaf, half a round of cheese, a comb, a razor and three bottles of our good Boisvert wine for which I have cleverly remembered to obtain a corkscrew. They had no sausage, to my regret, but there is here the tag end of a ham."

"It will do." Robert pawed in the basket. "We will need a knife. Did you not bring one?"

"*Ma foi!* That I did not remember."

Elizabeth picked up the razor and reached for the ham. "Never mind, this will do beautifully."

Robert howled and snatched the razor from her. "Good God, woman! You will dull the edge on that bone."

She looked at him helplessly. "But, my dear Robert, you cannot expect us to gnaw at it like a pack of hounds."

"Your scissors," he improvised. "We can cut chunks with one of the blades."

"And I shall require a new pair," Elizabeth muttered to herself as she turned her back to take out that much-abused tool. "I am far too hungry to argue with lunatics," she told him, handing over the scissors.

It was not easy to sever the ham from the bone, but Robert managed. The bread they broke into chunks, but the cheese had to be sawed into pieces with the scissors. Nevertheless, it was the best meal they'd enjoyed in days.

Armand had also forgotten soap for the razor, and only cold water from a horse trough outside was available. After several attempts and some lurid remarks in both languages, which Elizabeth was thankful she could pretend not to understand, both men decided against shaving. The château would have to receive them as they were. At least Elizabeth had combed her hair and hidden her disreputable bonnet in its hatbox.

Armand, though he brought a bottle of wine for each of them, had naturally neglected to bring glasses. Of necessity, they had been drinking directly from the bottles. Elizabeth failed to notice the disparity between a few ounces in a crystal container and the lowering level in her bottle. She sat and sipped while the men tried to shave outside, and when they gave up and came in, she continued to sip when they took up their own bottles.

Replete with their ham and cheese, they sat down in the hay to await Armand's friend, Gaston, and his wagon. Cheer now reigned, and to pass the time, they sang *"Alouette, je te plumerai,"* the one French nursery song they all knew. By the time the man came, they had deplumed the poor bird down to its toenails and depleted the wine.

Elizabeth, clutching her bottle and the hatbox, had to be hoisted into the back of the wagon with Robert beside her to steady her. He sat with his arms around her, strangely silent. Armand, having been weaned on the sole product of the region, proved to have a head impervious to alcohol, and sat with the driver chatting cheerfully. For her part, Elizabeth dozed as the wagon jolted along a deeply rutted lane.

She awoke when Robert exclaimed, "Good God!"

Opening her eyes, she gazed in awe at the Château de Boisvert.

No mansion as she had expected, but a medieval castle, built of the local stone, with crenellated roofs and turrets, all enclosed by a centuries-old wall and gate towers with arrow-loups for windows. And, of course, it had a moat—a wide one fed by a river that ran through the property. A massive drawbridge that must, when raised, have reached the top of the towers that guarded the gate, now served as a permanent bridge.

Muzzily, Elizabeth eyed the green slime on the water and the yellow-brown weeds along the shores as they rattled across the drawbridge. Near the middle of the moat, something blew bubbles, causing concentric ripples to widen over the sluggish surface.

She shuddered. More water. The way their luck ran, one of them would be bound to end up in that loathsome stream.

CHAPTER NINE

ROBERT SWALLOWED, his throat tight, bowled over by the magnificence of the estate that would be his if he married this unknown Frenchwoman.

The château was a cube, three storeys tall, with a higher square tower at each corner, and it stood on a small hill in the centre of walled grounds. Motte and bailey—the terms lingered in his brain from an otherwise forgotten course in the history of architecture at Oxford. He had never really expected to see an example. The motte, the hill on which the keep, the château itself, was constructed, would have been built up of the earth from the deep ditch that eventually became the moat.

The wagon entered through a massive iron gate set in the crumbling rock walls. Part of the original line of fortification, these enclosed the bailey, or courtyard. The picturesque ruins of a chapel and what must have been workshops, an armoury, a barracks and storehouses were now not much more than piles of rock overgrown with shrubs and flowers. A winding drive through a small stand of trees, past a rose garden and lawns, led up to terraced steps at the front entrance. Instead of stopping, their driver circled to the rear of the château, past an acre of tall hedges and a lake with a gazebo in its centre. He drew up at a great oaken portal crossed with black iron bars and secured with a latch that required man-size muscles to raise.

While Armand thanked the man and bade him farewell, Robert lifted Elizabeth from the back of the wagon, handed her the hatbox and relieved her of the empty wine bottle. After a moment's hesitation, he stowed it behind a handy bush.

Surprised at first, Elizabeth nodded sagely. "Yes, indeed. We must not have these people think me a drunkard."

She was weaving slightly, and he took a firm grip on her elbow. "Just do not attempt to speak," he ordered. "It will not be difficult, for I imagine all will be in French. I will explain what is said to you later," he added on a note of condescension that nearly, though not quite, prompted her to retaliate.

The wagon drove off, and Armand, with the ease of long practice, braced a knee against the door, pushed in with his shoulder and flipped up the heavy latch. He ushered them into a stone-paved, vaulted passage let through a wall at least ten feet thick.

The sudden chill inside sent a shiver through Elizabeth, clearing her head somewhat. "Good heavens, Armand," she remarked. "How old is this place?"

He beamed at her, flushed with pride. "Seven hundred years and more. It was mostly uninhabitable until the grapes and winery of my ancestor. Beneath us are the ancient cellars for the wine and cold rooms for the storage of meats and grains and vegetables. On this level we have the open rooms and above, bedchambers." He saw her face and hastened to add, "Do not fear for damp and the cold drafts. Inside, now, all is the most modern."

They were at the crossing of a passage, and a scullery maid hurrying by saw them. She let out a piercing shriek. "But you are a ghost!"

Armand caught her about the waist and planted a smacking kiss on her cheek. "Later, *mon petit chou,* I will show you how I am alive. Where are Oncle Gaston and Tante Marie?"

Before the girl could reply, they were surrounded by maids, cooks and footmen. To Elizabeth, there seemed to be dozens of domestics, all shouting at once in a veritable bedlam of rapid French. She flattened herself against the wall in the shadows. After several minutes of the pandemonium, her head ceased to spin so badly, and she sorted out the cast—Armand's uncle and aunt, who were the *maître* and *châtelaine* of the château, and a baker's dozen of underlings.

Armand's uncle and aunt welcomed him with open arms, kisses on both cheeks and shrieks of delight.

"Is it you, of a truth?" cried his aunt, tears streaming down her plump cheeks.

"But you are dead, Armand!"

"Dupont has arrived this day with the dreadful news!"

"Dupont!" Armand interrupted. "That pig is here?"

"He tells us you are lost at sea, and with you the long-lost English son of Georges! It is old Étienne who now claims to be the *comte!*"

"*Mais non!* Oncle Gaston, I have brought him. He is here. This is Robert, Comte de Boisvert!"

His announcement shocked the staff into a moment's silence. Then before he could dodge, Robert was forced to run a gantlet of hand kissing, bowing and curtsying, according to the rank of the delighted greeters.

Armand's aunt and uncle were all smiles. "Ah, but he will be pleased, our Étienne!"

"He has feared our family name to be at an end."

The babble broke out again.

"A celebration!"

"We must have a banquet!"

"Étienne must be notified at once! Pierre must go—saddle a horse!"

"No, hold!" Armand exclaimed. "Have you not had word from him? I sent a messenger on ahead."

"To Étienne?" Tante Marie raised her eyebrows and made a moue. "That one would not think to inform the staff at once. No doubt he comes in person to order all made ready to receive the new *comte*."

"Armand, you have not told. How came you to escape a certain death?" his uncle demanded.

Once more Armand was plied with questions.

Except for a few curious glances, Elizabeth had more or less escaped notice, the attention and excitement being riveted on Armand and the advent of the long-lost heir. She now came in for a torrent of queries, addressed not to her but to Armand, who explained that she did not speak French but was an Englishwoman, shipwrecked as they had been.

Being unused to so much wine, she still felt quite befuddled, and weary beyond belief, so she made no attempt to speak. Luckily, they attributed her blank expression and vague smiles to a lack of understanding of their words. She was soon thankful for her pretended ignorance of the language, for otherwise she would not have known where to look on hearing Armand's extravagant praises and seeing the admiring stares of his friends and relatives as he described their ordeal in the most flowery terms. Robert came in for his share of praise, and she noted that he tried to tone down Armand's version of his own exploits, and told instead of the few times the little Frenchman had really helped, playing down the disasters.

In the midst of his tale, a tiny, dark-haired girl hurtled into the passage. Tiny only in height, for her figure was rotund and sturdy. She was a veritable dumpling of a girl.

"Delphine!" cried Armand.

"My Armand!" she shrieked, and threw herself into his arms.

The whole story had to be told over and Robert and Elizabeth introduced again.

Delphine looked Robert up and down and shook her dark curls. "I do not want this English," she said flatly. "He is too big. Let him wed this other woman who clings to his arm and so obviously loves him."

Elizabeth understood her words only too clearly. She hastily dropped her grip on Robert's sleeve and turned away to hide her flaming face. Fortunately,

Delphine was once more kissing Armand and all eyes were on them.

Now that she was here where only French was spoken, Elizabeth had fully intended to reveal her knowledge of the language, but after this remark, she could not! She would never be able to face Robert if he knew she had heard.

Armand had come up for air. "Think, my beloved," he crooned to Delphine. "If you do not wed this new *comte,* all will belong to Étienne. We will have no home and be as paupers."

"Indeed not," Delphine told him in a tone that brooked no argument. "It is only that we must at once find the green fox of your mother. But why do we stand here in the cold and damp?"

She swept them all down the paved passageway to a cavernous room that must have been the original winter kitchen. Here it was warm indeed, for a fire blazed in a gigantic hearth built deep into an outside wall. Complete with hanging black iron pots, it also boasted a hand-wound spit that could turn a roasting sheep or even an ox with ease. All the walls were stone, but here they were cheery with whitewash, albeit permanently stained about the fireplace with the grease and smoke of ages past.

A great pine table, scrubbed white, ran down the centre of the room. In addition, every modern invention in the way of stoves and hot closets ranged between dry sinks and pantries about the sides. An open arch at one end revealed an efficient scullery.

Delphine took command at once. "The chambers of the *comte* for our new master," she decreed. "Move the effects of M. Étienne down the hall." Servants were sent on the run to prepare the rooms. "Armand, you will procure for the *comte* an outfit of dry garments from your own wardrobe, and have them sent to his dressing room. I myself will provide for the Mlle Garner and we will arrange for her the rooms next to myself."

Elizabeth, as yet not quite as sober as she could have wished, stifled a giggle at the expression on Robert's face. He seemed quite taken aback by this bossy female. The giggle nearly escaped as she thought of Armand. The Frenchman would have little chance of keeping his promise to that scullery maid while under the thumb of this domineering little woman.

"Brunot," Delphine continued, addressing Armand's uncle Gaston. "The state silver must be polished, for this evening we shall have a banquet. See to it." Tante Marie received more respect and the title of Madame Brunot. "I leave the menu to you, for you know best how to instruct Cook in the preparation of the proper viands. And now, *allons!* We go to escort the Comte de Boisvert to his chambers."

Armand, Elizabeth and Robert were carried off along another paved passage and through a pair of swinging double doors into the Great Hall of the château.

Elizabeth's first impression was of a dark, cavernous area stretching upward two storeys, the timbered ceiling disappearing into gloom above. The only light came through stone arches leading to rooms on the perimeter of the hall. Faded tapestries hung on the walls, no doubt in a vain attempt to counter draughts and dampness. Portraits of long-gone *comtes* glared down at her, and the gonfalons and pennants of past Foxes of Boisvert were draped from the railing of a gallery that ran around all four walls at the level of the next floor up. She could make out, though dimly, the outlines of doors to rooms on that storey.

And foxes. It seemed to her bemused eyes that there were foxes everywhere. Brass bowls and vases on heavy black oak tables were decorated with foxes. They were engraved on silver pitchers and trays. The great catches on the carved chests that stood between suits of armour by the stone arches were bronze fox heads. Moth-eaten fox masks mingled on the walls with the heads of wide-antlered deer of some sort, Elizabeth was not of a zoological turn. Antique weaponry covered the rest of the walls, and even there painted foxes snarled from battered shields, and tarnished silver foxes formed the hilts of crossed crusader swords mounted over the eight-foot-high mantel of a smoke-blackened hearth the size of a small room.

If they were to search out every fox in the château looking for one that was green, they might be here for years!

Their heels rang on the stone paving—except for Elizabeth's wool-wrapped foot. Delphine steered them up a wide, curving staircase with richly carved oak balusters. She turned to the left at the first landing, the gallery, and they walked towards the front of the château.

Elizabeth peered over the railing, down to the stone floor. Not fond of heights, she clung to Robert's hand until she encountered an approving glance from Delphine and moved back hastily to walk by Armand.

Two women ran past them, one loaded with a stack of gentleman's clothing, the other with a basket filled with more personal effects.

"Étienne's," Armand explained, his tone gloating. "He is a frequent visitor to the château, and is now being demoted to a guest room. So are the mighty fallen."

"I thought you said he did not wish to be the *comte*."

"He doesn't, but having had a taste of the quarters of a *comte,* he will not care for a Spartan guest cell."

"I don't care where I sleep, just so it has a bed." Her voice dreamy, Elizabeth went on. "Sheets, pillows, a soft pallet. Perhaps a warming pan and a fire. Oh, fudge!" She bent to catch the trailing end of her foot wrap. "I am once more coming apart. Do you suppose Delphine's generosity will run to a complete pair of slippers, or at least one more?"

She expected no answer and got none, for Delphine and Robert had reached the end of the gallery and stood before double doors, ornately carved with scenes involving, naturally, a number of foxes. As though at a signal, she and Armand ceremoniously threw open the portals and stepped back for Robert to pass through. Ever curious, Elizabeth followed.

Here, after the elegant austerity of the Great Hall, was opulence indeed. The late sun streamed in between heavy wine-velvet draperies thrown aside from mullioned windows. It shone on walls papered with red-and-gold Chinese silk, chairs covered in needlepoint in a rich pattern of purple iris and mauve cabbage roses, and gleamed on softly glowing dark mahogany. Bronze running foxes looped back hangings of cerulean brocade silk from the tester of a gigantic bed covered with a deep blue satin quilt embroidered with gold thread. A mahogany step stood ready to assist the sleeper to mount.

Robert, obviously more accustomed to luxury than she, wandered about the room, treading on exotic Oriental carpets. Ornaments and candelabra adorned every surface capable of holding them, and paintings covered much of the walls.

"Good God, what a mess," Robert remarked, looking about at the clutter.

He paused before a looming inlaid-mahogany wardrobe and opened the doors wide. It was empty.

"I have a memory," he said, turning to Armand, "of two beautiful words spoken below stairs. Dry garments."

"But of a certainty," Armand responded with alacrity. "For both of us. I have plenty."

"Then lead me to them. Where are your rooms?"

Armand's mouth twisted. "Not here, you may be sure. *Le salopard,* the by-blow, does not sleep with the nobility. On the death of my *grand-père, le comte,*" he added bitterly, "Étienne had me moved to the attics above, with *mon oncle* and *ma tante* and the rest of the servants."

Robert frowned. "I begin to dislike this Étienne."

The Frenchman's ready smile flashed. "You join a large company. You see now why all are so pleased that you are found."

"Lead on." Robert clapped him on the shoulder. "Let us also find these dry clothes."

The two men left, and Delphine turned to Elizabeth, speaking in laboured English. "This way we walk. To the room, no? For a gown not wet."

Obviously this was not the time to answer in perfect French and embarrass her hostess. Elizabeth merely nodded brightly and wondered when, if ever, she would find the right moment to confess. Oh, Scott was right when he wrote of tangled webs. Perhaps she could pretend to learn rapidly....

Delphine took her back round the gallery to the head of the hall stairs and continued on to the opposite side. Here she opened a pair of folding doors leading off at a right angle into a different wing entirely. Of course, it would not be the thing for unmarried young ladies to sleep in the same part of the building with bachelors.

They entered another gallery that ran around the back three wings of the square château. This one enclosed a courtyard, a quadrangle open to the sky. On the inner side were doors leading to chambers, on the other, overlooking the courtyard, were Gothic pointed-arch casement windows.

The first door opened on Delphine's bedchamber, a charming room in soft tones of green, but alarming in its neatness and order, for it told of a character far removed from Elizabeth's. Never had her own room been so tidy. She found herself looking about, wondering where Delphine actually lived.

Her hostess kept up a continuous commentary in French as she rummaged through the orderly display of gowns in her wardrobe. "Alas, this one is so tall! I do not own a gown that will not appear on her to be indecent, so much leg and bosom they will show. We must improvise. Not this, for it is my favourite—or the blue. Can I part with the green? Ah, this will do for dinner tonight." She selected a gown in a delicate shade of pink. "I do not care for so high a neckline. It does not fit me well and the colour is of the most insipid."

Oh, worse and worse, Elizabeth thought, feeling thoroughly uncomfortable. Why had she not confessed her knowledge of the language the minute she arrived? She accepted the gown with every sign of pleasure, which was easy because the colour was a favourite and became her excessively. As for the fit, it was fortunate that fashion called for the shortest of bodices.

The length was quite another matter. Holding it up, Elizabeth felt like a gawky schoolgirl until the ever-efficient Delphine unearthed a wide length of blond lace from her work-basket and soon had it basted in place around the hem. But slippers ...

"Ah," said Delphine. "We have here the problem. These English have so large the feet! I must beg a pair from Madame Brunot." She attempted to explain this to Elizabeth, who nodded and smiled, not caring whose shoes she wore, just so there were two.

The room assigned to her was next door to Delphine's, and equally as comfortable. They parted at the door and Elizabeth leaned against it, looking around. Her poor cloak was spread over a chair to dry by the fender of a crackling wood fire. The dents had been knocked from her hatbox, the worst of the dirt removed, and it rested on a trestle at the foot of a most inviting bed. She dropped the armful of clothing and hastened to ascertain the safety of her bonnet. Assured that it was there, she stripped off her filthy clothing and bathed as well as she could with the basin and jug of hot water on the washstand. She dressed slowly, luxuriating in the softness—and dryness—of the undergarments so thoughtfully provided by Delphine. Aye, Delphine.

It was the first time in days that Elizabeth had been parted from Robert, and she felt lost and alone. What would she do now? Robert, she was sure, intended to wed Delphine and claim this tremendous estate. How could it be otherwise? Oh, but she wanted suddenly to go home, back to England, to safety and security. After all she had gone through these past days—with Robert—she could not bear the thought of remaining in France while another woman became his wife.

But hope would not be gainsaid. They had promised to aid Armand in the search for his green fox. And if only he found it and eloped with Delphine . . . She completed her toilette and stowed the precious hatbox in the depth of the commodious wardrobe. She had best stop fantasizing.

She hesitated a moment, considering her future, and then retrieved the hatbox and hid it instead under the bed, pulling the quilt down to reach the floor.

By the time she found her way back to the Great Hall, the others had already assembled. Armand and Delphine interrupted an argument that sounded serious to greet her. Robert, who had been standing aside as though deep in thought, looked up, his eyes warm with blatant admiration.

Elizabeth felt herself blush, conscious at once of the flattering shade of the pink gown and of its inadequate bodice. She needn't have worried about the rotund Delphine's skirts gathered about her own slim figure with a long hair ribbon. Robert, she saw, was in worse case than she.

Armand was not a tall man, and his sleeves and breeches were too short for Robert. She had always known him to be excessively handsome in spite of his frequently green countenance and the growing stubble of black beard. Now, her vision coloured by her tumultuous feelings, she thought him magnificent even in this odd costume. His dignity and arrogant air had returned along with his healthy colour, and he appeared a top-lofty giant compared to the shorter Frenchman. She was almost afraid of him, no longer her Robert to be cared for and cuddled with, but every towering inch the Comte de Boisvert.

His eyes met hers with a look so blazing that she took a startled step back. Here in France, the lord of all he could survey, would he feel entitled to exercise his droit de seigneur? A rush of warmth enveloped her, bringing a vivid flush to her cheeks at the memory of those kisses in the barn. Was that incident a prelude of events to come?

Then he smiled, his old teasing grin, and everything fell into its proper place. She could smile back.

"What a set-out they have given me," he said. "A bedchamber, a dressing room with accommodation for a valet, and a private garde-robe that,

Armand tells me, drains into the river downstream from the moat. How are you situated, love?"

Before she could respond to his use of this upsetting endearment, the crunching of gravel on the drive outside heralded the arrival of a carriage. Armand rushed to a window.

"Zut alors!" he groaned. "It is Étienne."

CHAPTER TEN

AT FIRST SIGHT, the sharp-featured Étienne did not find favour with Robert. He was overdressed in the extreme of Continental style, his manner was cold and he wore a permanent expression of impatience. Worst of all, he was single-minded regarding the preservation of the Boisvert line. A nervous-looking gentleman's gentleman who accompanied him shrank into the shadows and spoke not a word.

Brisk and efficient, the diminutive Delphine wasted no time in informing Étienne that she did not wish to marry Robert. "I am glad you have come, M. Étienne, for I would have words with you."

He raised a chilly eyebrow. "Would you indeed? And before these people are presented to me?"

"Of a certainty, for my words are of the utmost importance."

He held back his arms to allow Brunot to divest him of a many-caped greatcoat. "To you, perhaps. Do not be importunate, child."

"I do not care for this English," she declared, unabashed. "He is too big and...and too English."

He brushed aside her words as though they were annoying gnats. "Where is this one who is the son of the missing Georges, the new Comte de Boisvert?"

Robert stepped forward. "Georges de Boisvert was my father. I have with me the documents of proof."

Étienne walked slowly round Robert, inspecting him as though considering a purchase.

He had not been wrong, Robert thought, when he likened his position to that of a new stallion for the Boisvert stable. Perhaps he should flex his not inconsiderable muscle and bare his teeth for inspection.

"I am not spavined, my dear sir," he said, gritting those teeth, "nor am I over at the knees, goose-rumped, straight in the shoulder or a wind-sucker."

Étienne had no time for levity. He tilted back his head in order to look down his impressive nose at the taller Robert. "So you survive. When Dupont came to me with the news of your drowning, I placed my trust in *le bon Dieu* to preserve for us the future of the House of Boisvert and not in the words of Dupont, who has less brain than a pigeon."

Turning away from the fuming Robert, he addressed Armand. "And you return from your chase of the wild goose—or should I say fox?"

Armand bristled. "What do you know of my affairs?"

"I know there is no lost treasure other than in your mind. The valuables of the château were listed in inventory before the Terror. All the Boisvert heirloom jewels, to which in any case *you* have no right, are accounted for." He dismissed Armand's claims with a disparaging wave of a manicured hand. "You waste your time. I know of your search, for Dupont has confessed all. He has thrown himself upon my mercy and will be dealt with when I decide on a suitable punishment."

When *he* decided! "I believe," said Robert, ice in his tone at the slur on Armand's birth, "that as the Comte de Boisvert, it is for me to make such decisions."

Étienne's eyes gleamed. "Ah, you have the spirit. That is good. I remain here this night, for tomorrow will come the other executors and our family priest for the wedding."

Robert's head came up. "But, my dear sir," he began. "I have decided—"

"Nonsense, boy, there is no decision for you to make. All is arranged." Imperiously, he turned to his silent valet. "Fouchet, my bags. Take them up to my room at once."

When the man hesitated, Étienne spoke curtly to Armand's uncle, Gaston, who had been hovering in the background. "Show him the way, then. He has not been here before." He turned to Robert. "You no doubt know how it is with the lower class these days. They no longer keep to their place." This last seemed aimed at Armand, whose lips tightened.

"My Henri," Étienne went on, an edge to his words. "Even he. After forty years, he has had the presumption to retire before I die! This new one..." He shrugged. "He has not Henri's skill at the tying of cravats."

He had been eyeing Robert up and down as he talked. Now he snapped his fingers at Armand. "You. See to it that he is taken at once to a tailor. You are always outfitted above your station—it might not be amiss if our new *comte* allows your tailor to make up a coat and some breeches in his size. These garments he wears are deplorable."

Armand's chin stuck out. "Then he'd best go to your man, for these deplorable rags are mine."

Delphine stepped in at once. With the air of long habit, she attempted to smooth the troubled waters. "His clothes are of no account," she said. "Of first importance is the dinner. Our good Brunot awaits only the signal to strike his gong.'' She gave it.

She settled the matter of protocol by taking Robert's arm and guiding him to the dining parlour, leaving Étienne to escort Elizabeth, and Armand to follow as he would. She placed Robert at the head of the table, disconcerting Étienne, who had forgotten for the moment that he was not to be the *comte*. She then proceeded to seat herself, as hostess, at the foot, leaving Étienne to pull out a chair on Robert's right. Elizabeth, diplomatically, sat with Armand on the other side.

Delphine's masterful usurpation of the duties of the host—that is, of the Comte de Boisvert—did not sit well with Robert, who had wanted the pleasure of demoting Étienne for himself. Was this a portent of the future? He was more and more determined not to marry the high-handed Delphine. But could any way be found out of the dilemma, short of handing all over to Étienne, to whom he had taken a powerful aversion? Everything rested on Armand's finding his treasure, and if it existed, Robert determined it would be found.

The reason for his determination quietly watched the scene, her face pale. His eyes met hers, and their unconscious yearning struck a spark. The answering flame that ignited in her eyes kindled a blaze that left him shaken. Not until he was actually faced with marriage to another—with parting from Elizabeth!—had he realized the true depths of his feelings. Hell and the devil confound it! He had developed a lasting passion for the wrong woman.

AFTER THE FIRST decent—nay, delectable!—meal she had had in days, Elizabeth retired to her room, but she was far too aware of what she had seen in Robert's eyes for sleep. She sat by her window playing the moment over and over in her mind. Could she have been mistaken? No! No woman could mistake the naked emotion that had struck a palpable blow to the depth of her being.

Ever since that kiss in the barn she had been in a daze of misery, realizing that she was in love with him and he intended to marry Delphine to save his vast inheritance from Étienne. Now, one look from his blazing eyes, and she had been transported. To paradise? Or to an everlasting hell, suspecting he shared her love but would not accept it! Or would he? She wanted—no, needed—to speak to him, to touch him, to affirm what she believed to be true.

It would have to wait for the morrow. She climbed into the first sumptuous bed she had known for days. Or nights, she corrected herself, smiling at the memory of those nights.

The smile faded. Her bedside candle had guttered out by itself before she could snuff it, leaving her in total darkness. An eerie sensation crept over her, as though she were being watched. Seven hundred years, Armand had said. How many people had slept in this room—in this bed—and even died in it? If ever a castle deserved to be haunted, this was the one.

Delphine had lent her a dressing gown, and Delphine was near. Elizabeth slipped out of bed as silently as she could so as not to alert any waiting wraiths in the dark corners and put it on. In moments, she was out in the gallery.

Pale moonlight shone in through the tall casements, creating odd shadows on the walls. Disoriented at first, she couldn't remember which door was Delphine's. Next to hers, but which way? Of course, the closest to the folding doors on the end of the gallery.

She tapped on the door, meaning to beg for company or at least another candle to ward off the long-dead spirits she was sure crowded all around her. She tapped again, louder. There was no answer.

Panic began to rise within her. *But I do not believe in ghosts,* she told herself firmly. *At least, I try very seriously not to,* she amended.

Delphine must be a heavy sleeper. Elizabeth gave up on tapping and pounded on the door. It was not latched and swung slowly open. She stepped quickly inside and over to the canopied bed.

It was empty. Delphine was not there. She was alone up here . . . in the dark. . . .

Robert! Where was Robert? In the other wing, at the front, over the Great Hall. She was in night-rail—she should change—but nothing would make her go back into that dark, haunted bedchamber! She ran blindly out into the lighter gallery and down to the folding doors.

They were locked for the night. To protect the young girls from marauding males? What about marauding spectres?

Back stairs—there should be stairs for the servants, and she remembered seeing another door at the far end of the gallery where it joined the next leg of the quadrangle. She fled back towards it, the filmy dressing-gown floating behind her, ghost-like.

This portal opened, revealing the head of a narrow flight of steps leading down into pitch blackness. And probably to the kitchens. She could find her way to the Great Hall from there and then up the front staircase to Robert's wing. And safety.

She made her way down cautiously, one hand on either wall. This was no time to fall and break a leg. As she reached the bottom, she became aware of a light in the dark ahead. Candle glow seeped into the stone-flagged passageway in which she stood. A doorway, and now she could hear a man's voice—a living human being. She hurried towards it, hearing the clink of bottle and glass—and men talking in French. It was an ancient door and the candlelight shone through a slanted crack where it sagged away from the frame. About to make herself known, she stopped, her hand already reaching for the latch.

In one of those voices, she recognized the guttural tones of Dupont. He was answered unmistakably by the boatman, Gérard. But what were they doing here? As she listened avidly, a third voice broke in, raised in querulous tones that were oddly familiar. Then she placed it. The third man was the complaining brigand from the forest!

Creeping to the crack in the door, she peeked in—and had a clear view of Étienne's new valet. So *he* was the man whose horse they had borrowed—or rather commandeered—and in the employ of Étienne!

She eavesdropped shamelessly, and their conversation was well worth hearing.

Gérard gave a high-pitched exclamation. "*Non!* We will not pay you another franc! You did not keep your part of the bargain. The deal was that you delivered Armand into our hands and that did not happen."

The querulous voice whined again. "You did not tell me they would be armed and they were three to my one! I am surely due for a share, if only for my sore feet. They forced me to walk through half the Bois Vert. This time I will not fail."

"*We* will not fail. What makes you think you deserve any part?"

"Wait, Dupont." This was Gérard. "You forget an important point. He knows of our scheme."

Dupont growled. "Not for long."

"Wait!" Now it was the valet. "You owe me a favour. Had I not been present when M. Étienne received the message from Armand of their miraculous escape from drowning, you would never have known. Did I not warn you before you walked directly into the arms of the law for attempted murder?"

Gérard spoke thoughtfully. "It occurs to me that we might have use for this man. We are hunted men. He is the only one of us whose face may be seen in Boisvert. You heard Armand on the island. He would not have said he must return to the château if he did not know the fortune for which we search is here."

"But how did he know it was not on the island? They looked only at the lake."

"Did you not listen? Something he remembered out of the blue. Believe me, it is here. The château must be searched from attics to cellars, and for that we must have a free hand. There is where Fouchet comes in.''

Dupont made a disparaging noise. ''How?''

''He will be of the greatest help, for he will lure those three, one at a time, to some quiet place.''

''For what purpose?'' The valet's voice was uneasy.

''Purpose? Why, to clear the decks. Once Armand has led us to his treasure, it would be best no witnesses were left.''

Elizabeth, her ear glued to the crack in the door, nearly sank to her knees.

The valet's reaction was much the same. ''*Non!* I will not assist in such a scheme! I agreed only to deliver to you Armand, in good condition, not to become involved in a mass assassination!''

''Consider, my dear Fouchet.'' Gérard's words grew silky and suggestive. ''This new *comte* has stolen your master's rightful title.''

''He does not want it!''

''Aye, but you have not thought. It is a far cry from being the valet of a common *monsieur* to that of gentleman's gentleman to a *comte*.''

''It is not a position to kill for. Leaving those ones to possibly drown when by dint of some ingenuity they might escape—that I could condone—it is not the same as deliberate, cold-blooded murder.''

Elizabeth could quite see his point and warmed a bit to this Fouchet.

Not so Dupont. "Methinks we no longer need this coward," he snarled. "Let me but silence him."

Fouchet's voice rose in terror. "Keep him from me!"

"Hold, Dupont," ordered Gérard. "We will have corpses enough. Let him go."

"Indeed, yes! I go at once." Fouchet must have been inching towards the door already, for his voice had become louder.

"The moat is deep," said Dupont.

There came a brief scuffling, and the door burst open before Elizabeth could retreat. She and Fouchet stared at each other for a few seconds before her quick mind functioned. She must not recognize him from the forest—after all, his face had been hidden then by a scarf.

"Oh," she exclaimed, managing to sound relieved. "You are the valet of M. Étienne, are you not?" She smiled brightly. "Please, do you speak English? I am lost in these halls and cannot find the stairs to my room."

He recovered his composure and bowed. "It is that way, *mademoiselle*," he said in stilted English, and pointed down the stone passage. "I would guide you, but I go a different path. You must pardon me. It is that I have received an urgent call from the south of France—the farthest south to which I can get.''

He took off at a run, and Elizabeth, knowing her voice had been heard by the men inside the room, followed suit, in the other direction.

She had to warn Armand and Robert! She did not know where Armand slept, but she knew Robert would be in the chambers of the *comte,* at the end of that long and dark gallery. As she ran past the kitchens, she spotted a glow from one of the banked fires. She paused long enough to locate a candle and blow a hot coal into flame to light it. Locating the latch on the double baize doors that divided the servants' area from the Great Hall, she slipped through. The candle lit her way to the front staircase, but before she reached the gallery it proved a detriment.

Elizabeth had a far too active imagination, and the candle created weird shadows that seemed to move as though the suits of armour had come to life. She mounted the steps in record time. Étienne must have rooms up here—suppose he heard her footsteps and came out! She tried to make herself tiptoe along the dark gallery to Robert's chamber. With the thought of safety and security in his arms, she began to hurry, endangering the flame of her candle. It wavered, sending a blacker shadow running after her. A ghost? Or even worse, had one of those murderous men followed her?

Her nerve shattered, she pelted down the gallery. When she reached Robert's door, she pounded on it in panic, then turned to confront the demon who pursued her. The gallery, now that she held her candle almost still, settled into merely a long, dark corridor.

Her wildly beating heart began to slow—until Robert opened the door behind her. She turned, and they were face to face, alone in the night. The shock of awareness that vibrated in the air held them in its spell.

Robert had been thinking of Elizabeth and that kiss in the barn. What might have happened if that scene had gone on? He could never trust himself alone with her again. Then, he had stopped at the kiss, so stunning had been the revelation that he was in love. He was not at all sure he could stop another time if they met alone under such circumstances. And here she stood, come to him in the night, in a negligée and fetching lace cap that could only have come from Paris. His breath caught. She was lovely in the soft light from the candle she held. A flicker of startled surmise glinted in his eyes and vanished the next moment, for hers held only lingering fright—and trust.

Instead of taking her in his arms and claiming her on the spot, he held out a hand that shook with the effort of his control. "Why have you come? You shouldn't be here, Elizabeth. I—I am not safe for you to be with."

She stood her ground. Though every instinct urged her to run...or stay...she fought free of her trance.

"We are none of us safe, Robert. Those men plot to kill us!" Her words tumbling over themselves, she told him of listening to the conspirators.

"How could you listen? They must have spoken French."

"I have been meaning to tell you," she began with a guilty, sidelong glance. "I am quite fluent in French."

"What! Why did you not say so?"

"It...it seemed the best idea at the time. You see, Armand said—that is, I understood too well some of his words, and it would have quite put me to the blush to admit it."

"I remember." His tone was grim.

"Yes," she said eagerly. "Then you do see. And once started, I knew not how to confess."

"Humph. Well. Be that as it may. Begin at the beginning and tell me all." She followed him meekly as he took the candle from her and led her to a chair by the hearth—as far as possible from his tumbled bed. He listened without comment as she poured out her story in detail.

"So, our good Étienne is once more without a valet," he said when she finished. "A pity." He rose. "Come, we'd best waken Armand and hold a conference."

"Yes, indeed. Had I known where to find his rooms, I would have gone to him, as well."

Robert stopped. "You would, would you?"

She saw the pit and teetered on the rim. "Only with you. I would never go to a man's chamber alone."

"I see. Then you do not think me a man? I could show you—" He paused because she was laughing.

"You tease me, sir—I mean, Comte. If you know the way to his room, let us hurry." Her light mood died. "I truly believe he is in danger. They mean to force him to disclose the whereabouts of his treasure and may already have made a move."

Picking up the candle, he took her by the hand. The candlelight wavered as they walked down the gallery and up another flight of stairs, but not a single shadow followed them.

Robert knocked loudly on Armand's door and opened it immediately.

That gentleman was already awake, sitting on the edge of his bed, facing Delphine, who occupied his only chair.

Robert raised his brows. "In England," he told her sternly, "this would mark the end of our betrothal."

"Good," she said calmly. "Are you come to challenge Armand to the duel?"

"No, no," Robert assured her. "I am all for it."

She nodded briskly. "Then let us be done with that foolishness. Have you come to catch us thus to end it?"

Robert seemed inordinately cheerful. "You are fair and far off that road," he said. "We have come to try to save our skins. Elizabeth has a tale to unfold."

Believing it best to get over rough ground as lightly as possible, Elizabeth decided to explain her knowledge of French at once. Besides, she had just thought of a splendid excuse for deceiving them.

"I have not spoken before," she said, "because I learned your language in the schoolroom and was in terror of uttering some frightful gaffe and making a fool of myself."

She was assured, almost sincerely, that her pronunciation and accent were perfect. Armand, looking thoroughly abashed, seemed to feel an apology might be in order.

"Had I known—" he began.

Elizabeth shook her head. "Do not concern yourself, my friend. I speak only the classical French and could not understand much that was said."

"Enough," said Robert, who had been trying frantically to remember his own words in the boat, on the island and during the pouring rain in the woods. "Tell them what you overheard."

Elizabeth repeated her story. "And so," she ended, "it must be Étienne who is behind all."

This Armand denied vehemently. "Étienne is not a likable character," he conceded, "but the man is painfully honest and a fanatic. To him, only carrying on the bloodline of the Boisverts matters. It is that these scoundrels, his valet and Dupont, seek my treasure."

As was her custom, Delphine took charge. "Then we must find it first, but we must wait until daylight. Nothing can be done in the dark."

Oh, can it not? Robert tried to catch Elizabeth's eye, but she watched Delphine, all innocence.

"En effet," said Armand, "it is of the first importance to find my green fox. I must have the treasure so I can elope with Delphine before she is forced to marry Robert. I am sorry if it means you will not inherit the château, *mon ami,*" he added, "but I was not making the joke when I said I would

be cast out into the streets by Étienne. I have been a matter of contention between him and my *grand-père* since my birth.'' His usually cheerful features had that bitter twist Elizabeth had seen before. ''Étienne does not believe bastards should be recognized by their betters.''

Robert said what he would like to do to Étienne. But under his breath, unfortunately. Elizabeth thought it sounded interesting.

This had thrown another light on the matter for Robert, who realized with a sinking feeling that he had little faith in this treasure of Armand's. If it existed at all, in an estate of this size it would be impossible to find. He would be the cause of Armand and Delphine's being cast penniless into the streets, and unless he fulfilled the terms of the will, they would be. But what else could he do? He rose from the edge of the bed where he had been sitting and strode about the room silently.

CHAPTER ELEVEN

ELIZABETH'S HEART lurched sickeningly at Armand's words. Certainly Robert would wed Delphine. She had always suspected he meant to do so in the end. One had only to see the vast estate that would be his to realize he could have no other choice. How could she ever hope to compete with such wealth?

She received unexpected help from Delphine

"No," said that damsel. "I do not wish to marry Robert and this other one does. Let her take him. We shall discover this green fox of Armand's mother and all will be well"

Elizabeth felt honour bound to demur. "But if you elope with Armand, what will happen to Robert's inheritance? Will all go to Étienne?"

"Of that you may be sure."

In spite of her better judgement, Elizabeth's spirits rose. Would he then return to England? And turn for solace to her? She was being nonsensical.

She came back to earth. Delphine was speaking in her usual forceful tone. Robert stared into space, looking sombre, and Armand hung on his beloved's every word.

"We must decide the method of operation that no time be wasted," she decreed. "Let us work out a plan. First, we need not search within the château."

This brought a yelp from Armand. "But it is here! It must be!"

She smiled at him kindly, as though about to pat him on the head. "No. But listen again to the words of your mother, *mon coeur*. 'Look for it in the island where the green fox rises from the water. To the left, always to the left.' In themselves, the words of the clue eliminate such foxes as appear on door knockers and table silver, for these items lack both water and islands."

Thank goodness, Elizabeth thought, looking round Armand's chamber. Foxes were everywhere, on his dresser pulls, the backs of his brushes, on a silver-and-crystal box that held his rings and neckcloth pins. One even formed the handle of the shaving mug on his washstand.

"But, Delphine—"

"No buts." Delphine was adamant. "We must now turn our eyes to the grounds without. I did not believe in your Île de Renard. While you were absent, to satisfy my mind, I searched the château with the thoroughness of a hungry mouse scenting a crumb. In vain. Even both secret passages are empty of all but cobwebs, except for the skeleton under the west wing.''

''Skeleton!'' This commanded Elizabeth's wandering attention.

Delphine shrugged. ''We do not know who it was. A robber, perhaps.''

Elizabeth was scandalized. ''Why have you not buried the poor man?''

Armand grinned at her. ''What, should we remove such a deterrent to future housebreakers? He serves a purpose.''

Indeed. A deterrent to Elizabeth. She resolved on doing no explorations of the château. Remembering the black shadow that had pursued her along the gallery, she shuddered. His ghost—demanding interment?

Robert voiced an objection. ''Surely Armand's father would have kept his treasure close at hand where he could guard it.''

''I have already considered that,'' said Delphine. ''And it has occurred to me that it may not have been the father who laid away the treasure. I think the mother, when hearing of his death, may have secreted it to save for her son. We have only her words, not his.''

''Then, where . . . ?''

''She was a domestic, not of the nobility. It would be far more in character for her to hide it where *she* could keep it out of view.''

Robert, who had been sitting on the bed by Armand again, sprang up. "The kitchens."

Delphine looked smug. "The first place I searched."

Somewhat grumpily, he sat back down.

The speculations went on and on. Elizabeth became conscious of an unbelievable headache and a queasy stomach. She had drunk far more wine during the past few days than in her life before. And there had been more at dinner, with Étienne proposing numerous toasts. However had Robert managed to be heroic while seasick if his insides churned like this? Her admiration for him grew.

She met Robert's eyes, and what she saw there set her heart pounding. The blood rushed to her cheeks, and she turned away quickly, moving over to the window. They had retired very late, Étienne having been desirous of relating the entire history of the Boisverts to the new heir. It was now dawn and already the first rays of the rising sun glinted on the moat below.

Her attention was drawn by what appeared to be a dancing spray of water in the midst of the acre of tall hedges they passed on their way to the château. As she puzzled over what it could be, she became aware of Robert's eyes still upon her. Disconcerted, she hurried into speech, saying the first thought in her head. "Can that be a fountain out there?"

Delphine was at her side in an instant. She stared out the window and said a few words in incomprehensible French that caused Robert to look at her sharply.

"I have been a fool!" she exclaimed. "I did not remember, but there is a fox, carved in green marble, adorning that fountain in the centre of the maze!"

"But yes!" Armand cried. "It is my clue, for why else would my mother say to me 'To the left, always to the left,' which is the key to the maze."

Delphine threw her arms about his neck and kissed him soundly. "Of course, that is it! A pool of water surrounds the fountain and the statue of the fox rises from it!" She pushed them towards the door. "Let us make haste. The executors of the will, and worst of all the priest, are due this afternoon. Only think of the trouble saved if we succeed before they arrive!"

Their hearts full of hope, they parted to dress, not wishing to shock any early risers by cavorting about the fountain in their nightwear. They agreed to meet in the Great Hall as quickly as possible.

Ten minutes later, having donned her garments—or rather Delphine's—more rapidly than ever before in her life, Elizabeth was about to lock her door. She hesitated. Those evil men had said they would search the château from attics to cellars. Mere door locks might not stop them. It was not safe to leave her hatbox in her room. Suppose they had already been here?

In sudden fear, she ran back inside and peered under her bed. The box was still there. But her bonnet? She yanked off the lid and sat back in relief. Her poor hat was intact. She could not leave it behind. Draping the loop over her arm, she took it with her. Now they could search all they wished. In her room they'd find only her ruined gown and drying cloak. And one boot. Let them make of that what they would.

DOWN IN THE GREAT HALL, Robert paced restlessly, hungry for the sight of one special figure. She came, and his pulse picked up its tempo. How adorable she looked in that too-short gown—and with her ridiculous hatbox hung over her arm!

"Why the devil did you bring that?" he demanded.

Elizabeth hesitated, as though hunting for a logical excuse. She found one.

"Sentiment, I daresay. It has been with me through all our adventures. Surely it deserves to be in at the end."

"Women!" he said fondly, shaking his head. "There is no understanding them."

But it was good to discover this indomitable female had a soft and sentimental side. Now if only she felt the same towards one human who had accompanied her on that journey... and if only that journey could reach a happy conclusion for Armand and Delphine, as well.

Before he could speak again, they were joined by the other couple and hustled out by a side door in the dining parlour.

The way to the entrance to the maze took them along the green, slime-covered moat. Below four-foot banks, the water flowed sluggishly, the yellowish grasses and mossy plant life waving slowly like tentacles.

Elizabeth's premonition of the previous day returned in force. She shuddered and moved to the other side of the group. Something of Robert's revulsion of water must have rubbed off on her. It was a relief to reach the tall, thick hedges bordering the maze.

The hedges were high, at least six feet, and seemed an impenetrable wall until they came to two yew trees, sentinels on either side of a break in the shrubbery.

Leaning against one of them was a stout, oaken pole some seven feet long and topped with a faded red flag.

Armand picked it up, carrying it before him like a spear. "We had best bring this along."

Elizabeth's uneasiness lingered, and she glanced back over her shoulder. "For a weapon? Do you think we may need one? Suppose those men see us go in here."

The Frenchman laughed. "They may see for all the good it will do them. Once we are inside, I defy anyone to find us."

"That is why he brings the flag," said the pragmatic Delphine. "Wanderers hopelessly lost in these myriad passages may be easily located by someone outside who can be signalled with it."

"By all means bring your flag!" said Robert, who had once been lost in the maze at Hampton Court.

Elizabeth was not so easily put off. "I worry more about our being found than our being lost. Armand, after all, knows the key."

This seemed to Robert an excellent excuse to put a comforting arm about her. He did so. "You are being nonsensical, love. Looking for trouble."

There, he had called her that again. But it could mean nothing. Oh, perhaps a fondness from their close association—but worth testing further.

"Everywhere I look I imagine I see Dupont or that Gérard," she suggested hopefully. It worked. The reassuring arm developed into a hug.

"If you are concerned," Armand told her, "let us hide ourselves at once." He herded them all into the maze and guided them rapidly round several random turns. "There," he announced happily. "No one will ever be able to find us now."

"I see," said Robert, stopping suddenly. "And will we be able to find ourselves?"

"Of a certainty. Remember the key. To the left, always to the left."

Robert raised his brows. "From what point? Have you any idea where we are now?"

Armand's mouth dropped open and he clapped a hand to his forehead. "*Mon Dieu,* I did not think. We should have begun to turn left from the entrance!"

"Are you telling us," Elizabeth asked ominously, "that we are already lost in this maze?"

"Never fear," he assured her. "We have the flag. Someone will find us."

"Yes. Dupont or Gérard! Keep it down."

The path they followed dead ended ahead with turns to either side like the top of a T.

"Ah," said Armand happily. "Now we may begin. To the left, always to the left."

"He could be correct," Elizabeth grudgingly admitted. "Indeed, I fancy I can hear the splash of the water fountain in that direction."

Robert shook his head. "All the more reason to go the other way. The design of a maze is to be contrary and deceive the walker. We shall go to the right."

Armand insisted on taking the left turn. "It is my clue."

"He is correct," said Delphine in her most dictatorial manner. "We go left."

As Elizabeth expected, Robert's hackles rose. He was not one to take orders from a female. *Del-*

phine is handling him all wrong, she thought. *It will be a miserable marriage! I could do so much better, had I the chance.*

"I believe we should turn right," he said predictably.

"Left," said Delphine.

Unexpectedly, Robert grinned. "Go your way, we shall go ours."

"No!" Elizabeth exclaimed, forgetting at the first crisis how to manage him. "We should not separate!"

"Do not worry," Robert told her. "We can shout, and Armand can wave his flag." He led Elizabeth off, and Delphine and Armand went the other way.

"This may be the best," they heard Delphine tell him. "Who knows which of us might reach the centre first? Two are better than one."

Elizabeth agreed, especially if she should be the one, and Robert made up the two. Oh, why did he have to be noble and marry to save the skins of Armand and Delphine?

They wandered for some time in silence, up one passage and round more turns. The sound of the splashing water faded away, but Elizabeth heard other noises—stealthy sounds like footfalls or someone brushing against the solid hedges near them. She gripped Robert's arm.

"Are we being followed?" she asked in a whisper.

As if in answer, they heard a voice from the other side of the shrubbery. Armand's voice.

"Delphine, my love," he was saying. "Come here." There was a short, pregnant pause. "My own, I would that priest was coming for us." His words sounded muffled, as though spoken into her hair. "What if we do not after all find my fortune? Will you then run away with me?"

Her answer came quite clear. "Do not be ridiculous, Armand. This time we cannot fail. The treasure will be here."

"That I know." Another pause, no doubt for another kiss. "I merely ask to test your love. Would you not go with me, no matter what occured?"

"No, Armand, that cannot be. I could not be the wife of a poor man. I have not been bred to accept that role. But do not despair, it is but a marriage of convenience. Once I have borne him a son and heir, I will be free to take a lover, and he shall be you, my Armand."

Armand still had a problem. "Suppose your children are all girls?"

"I will make only a boy." And such was the power of her character that none of her three listeners thought to doubt her.

During a longer pause, Robert murmured in Elizabeth's ear, "You see how she plans to deceive me." He tilted up her chin with one finger. A devil lurked in his dancing eyes. "Elizabeth, I don't suppose..."

"No, indeed." She pulled him away to where they could no longer overhear the lovers. "You must not tease me so, Robert. It is most improper."

He sobered in an instant. "It is my intention that all will become perfectly proper."

"Of course." She turned away. He was to marry another woman, and she should not allow him to dally with her. Gentlemen, she knew, were not above such actions. Truly, now that their adventure was so nearly over, he was becoming a most dangerous man.

She faced him again. "I will not be any man's mistress. I have not been bred to accept that role, to quote your future bride."

"She is not my future bride," he said, his voice rough. He swept her into his arms. "Ever since I kissed you in that barn, I've known I could not go through with that marriage."

Though her heart was beating so hard that she could barely speak, Elizabeth held back. She had to be sure. "Robert, what are you saying?"

"What do you think I'm saying? I've tried— God, how I've tried!—to convince myself you were but a passing fancy, but I find I am singularly hard to convince. Elizabeth, I want you."

"What . . . what for?"

"Damn it, Elizabeth, do not play dense. I am trying to ask you to marry me!" He crushed her to him, his lips found hers and she was lost to the world.

When she came to her senses, Elizabeth brought up the problem that faced them. "Robert, Étienne cares only to have found a *comte* capable of carrying on the title. I cannot see him turning over this vast estate to you out of the goodness of his heart. If you do not fulfil the requirements of that ghastly will, what will happen to Armand and Delphine?"

"To the devil with that money-conscious pair. I have now lost all sympathy for them. Put down that confounded hatbox so I may kiss you properly."

As soon as she could speak again, Elizabeth reminded him of all he stood to lose. "Robert, you are giving up incredible wealth!"

"I do not give a straw for gold," he said, kissing the tip of her nose. "Unless it matters to you. To quote Delphine again, is it that you cannot be the wife of a poor man? Elizabeth, could you not live with me in a pauper's cottage until I can get a letter of credit sent to me by Mr. Breckenridge?"

She feared he would regret giving up his fabulous inheritance later, but this was not a moment to spoil. He loved her. She sighed happily, her hands on his cheeks, and drew his lips down to hers, willingly grasping this bit of heaven.

Sometime later, they became aware once more of stealthy sounds from the passage next to theirs. Elizabeth raised her head from his shoulder. "Our companions approach," she murmured.

"Ignore them," said Robert, and returned to the business at hand. The sounds continued... footsteps, rustlings in the shrubbery.

They were once more interrupted, this time by a shout from Armand, coming from the opposite direction to the noises they were hearing.

Robert straightened, setting her gently aside. "Those are not our friends on the other side of this hedge."

Armand shouted again. "Come! We have found it!"

The muted sounds near them ceased, replaced by the crashes of someone clearing a way through a jungle—heading towards Armand's voice.

"That is definitely no friend!" exclaimed Robert. He took off at a run.

Armand's flag was waving somewhere ahead; Elizabeth caught up her hatbox and dashed after Robert, down first one passage, then another.

When they reached Armand and Delphine by the fountain, the jungle clearer was hacking through the hedges behind them. He burst through. Dupont—and in his hands a double-headed axe from the weapons on the walls of the Great Hall.

His wild-eyed gaze centred on Elizabeth, who was clutching her hatbox to her breast. He advanced upon her triumphantly, the axe raised, threatening her with instant extinction.

He spoke in a near whisper. *"The treasure!"* He extended his other hand. *"Mademoiselle,* you will give me that."

"Stand off," Robert ordered.

Dupont turned on him and took a vicious swipe with the axe.

"Robert! No!" Elizabeth screamed in terror. He would be killed!

But he dodged and snatched the heavy flag pole from Armand to parry the blow. Dupont hefted the axe. Robert held the staff at the ready. They circled, two snarling dogs on the lookout for an opening. Robert thanked the powers that be for the hours he had trained at single stick while in fencing instruction, but wished they had rather been spent with the quarterstaff.

"I'll take you first." Dupont made another swipe with the axe and missed. "Then the others." He swung again, but the axe was heavy, solid iron, and he was already panting from demolishing the hedges on his way through the maze. "It will ... be years before ... your bodies are found. This maze ... is not much used."

Robert saved his breath for knocking aside the axe. He managed to fend off half a dozen blows, but deep chips were cut from the flag pole.

Elizabeth wisely refrained from screaming again. Anything might distract him. She held back Armand, pressing him against the hedge. Delphine only watched, for once helpless.

Then Robert saw the opening he waited for, and cracked Dupont's fingers between the oaken staff and the axe handle.

The man howled and the axe went flying. Still howling and hugging his broken hand, Dupont charged back through the holes he had hacked in the hedge. They heard him crashing his way about in the puzzling turns of the maze until he must at last have found an exit.

In the silence that followed, Elizabeth suffered a sudden reaction and turned on Robert. Out of control, her vocal cords skidded an octave. "You might have been killed!"

He touched her face with a tender finger. "I am safe, love," he told her gently. "I had no intention of letting him crack my skull with that axe."

"Enough," said Armand. "Dupont is halfway to the village by now." He rubbed his hands together. "Let us retrieve my fortune."

CHAPTER TWELVE

FOR THE FIRST TIME, Elizabeth really looked at the fountain at the heart of the maze. Awestruck, she counted off the required points of Armand's clue: a pool of water, surrounded by a low, grey marble rim; in the middle, a sort of island thrust upward, created of yellow-streaked stone; white alabaster fish poking up their heads about its base, squirted water on a green marble fox posed on the island as though he had just leapt out.

It could not be more right.

Armand had already shed his boots. They stood behind him, rather like a colour guard, as he drew a deep breath. Delphine received the coat he removed, folding it ceremoniously over her arm. Elizabeth felt as though she attended a coronation or perhaps the unveiling of a priceless painting. Armand stepped into the foot-deep water and advanced on the tiny island.

Half an hour later, Armand sat on the rim of the pool, soaking wet and pallid with dismay. Delphine, at his side, seemed for once stunned into silence.

"Someone has beaten us to it," Elizabeth said, knowing her words held no comfort.

Armand raised a lugubrious face. "*Non.* That cannot be. I have covered every inch. There is not a nook or cranny big enough to hold anything larger than a water snail."

"Gems do not come much bigger."

"That I thought of, so I looked in every hollow. And neither could I find a door or a lid or any bit that could turn or come apart. The stone is smooth and solid. Even that...that beast has closed the mouth. My treasure is not here."

Robert walked about the pool, running his hands through his hair.

"Damn," he said, a mild expletive, considering the ruin of all their hopes.

Delphine roused. "I do not believe there ever was a treasure. We have laboured under a delusion, a figment of our imagination."

"My mother would not lie. Somewhere it exists." Armand was not one to remain disheartened for long. Needing a safety valve to release his emotions, he looked about for a scapegoat and settled on Dupont. "*Nom de chien,* only see how that *salopard* has ruined our so beautiful maze." He picked up the axe, hefting it grimly. "Only let that *cochon* show his face in Boisvert again!"

"It will soon grow once more," Elizabeth soothed, relieved to see him showing spirit.

"I will not be here to see it."

Delphine squared her plump shoulders and took the baton from Elizabeth. "You are wet. It is not easy for the morale to lighten when one's clothing is sodden. Come, we go home—" her voice caught for a second "—we go to the château for dry garments."

To leave the maze was easy, now that they were at the centre, merely a matter of reversing the key. To the right, always to the right. They emerged from an exit beside the moat.

Gérard awaited them there. He had armed himself with a rusted broadsword torn from the display on the walls of the Great Hall. Half-mad with fury, he straddled the path.

"So," he hissed. "That idiot Dupont has failed again. Be assured I will not."

His eyes, like Dupont's, went straight to the hat-box Elizabeth still clutched to her breast.

"I will take that." Melodramatically, he menaced Elizabeth with the sword. "You will hand it to me if you value your life."

"Not again!" Robert might be contemptuous of her taste in bonnets, but he was not about to have his Elizabeth once more threatened by a misguided assassin. After the emotional scenes he had just gone through, he lost his patience. Remembering he carried the chipped oaken flag pole, he jabbed the importunate villain in the ribs.

Gérard knocked the pole away with the sword. Robert's adrenaline still flowed from the altercation with Dupont and he brought his substitute quarterstaff to defence position—barely in time to deflect a savage swipe.

The moat was behind him. Parrying the slashing attack, Robert circled until it was at the other man's back, not his own. He was not about to be driven into that ominous water.

Gérard being no swordsman, Robert was successfully holding him off, but Elizabeth had had enough. "Armand," she cried. "Help him!"

Armand had Dupont's axe.

Robert saw him come behind Gérard, preparing a mighty chop at the back of the boatman's knees, and he yelled in horror.

"Good God! Armand, no!" Momentarily sidetracked, he barely avoided a tremendous swing of the rusty sword.

Armand shrugged and reversed the axe. Seeing an opportunity, he thrust the handle between Gerard's legs and forked him over the bank and into the moat with a mighty splash. The slimy water closed over the boatman's head.

Dropping the staff, Robert stared down at the spreading ripples in the water, the horror of his nightmare returning in full . . . the crushing weight of the black water . . . unseen coiling tentacles wrapping about his legs, pulling him under . . . his lungs bursting . . . the most hideous of deaths! He could not let the man drown!

Gérard came up, splashing desperately. Slipping and sliding, Robert went down the bank, extending his hand as far out as he could reach.

Gérard managed to grab it in a viselike grip—and with his other hand, he grabbed Robert's ankle. Bracing his feet against the bank, he yanked, jerking Robert out over his head and into the moat.

The green water closed over his head. Robert's control deserted him, and he was engulfed in the mindless panic of his nightmare. But not for long. Armand's words rang in his ears. "Any person can swim! Be the dog! Chase the cat!"

His arms and legs pumped furiously, pursuing that elusive feline. Amazingly, he moved through the water without sinking.

Breaking the surface, he gasped in a lungful of air, just in time to be struck on the head by the battered flag pole extended towards him by Armand.

He went under again and fought his way up, buoyed by a mixture of anger at Armand and a crazy desire to laugh. Not, he realized to his surprise, with abject fear. He *could* be the dog! He could *swim!* Ignoring the staff, he held up his nose and paddled to the bank where eager hands seized him and pulled him onto land.

He stood, feeling ten feet tall. He dripped green water and assorted rotting river flora, but his soul soared in triumph. He had faced his enemy and won.

Elizabeth threw her arms about him, giving him a fervent hug and soaking her gown with slimy water. "Robert, you swam! You really swam!"

He turned to the moat, sneering at his defeated foe. As he looked past the undulating grasses at its edge, the sluggish water heaved and swelled in a gentle surge, breaking free of a floating dam of swamp debris churned up from the bottom by the recent action. The raft of debris rose and fell, rose and fell.

Robert's queasy stomach turned over, and he swallowed back a wave of nausea. Being able to chase a cat through water like a dog had nothing to do with getting seasick.

Armand touched his slimy shirt, wrinkling his nose. "You are very hard on my wardrobe, *mon ami*. I at least bathed in the cleaner fountain."

Robert looked back at the sluggish opaque water. The ripples had passed and the surface remained unbroken. An unpleasant thought struck him.

"Gérard," he whispered.

Armand shrugged. "Gone."

"Gone..."

Robert straightened up. Could he jump in again? There was always a chance he was not too late. He drew a deep breath, steeling himself for the task.

"Gone," Armand repeated cheerfully. "Right after he pulled you in, he climbed out and ran. I do not think he will return. We are witnesses to attempted murder.''

Delphine relieved her feelings in her usual form by scolding. ''You must both come in at once and don dry clothing. We are already very late for breakfast.''

Breakfast! Elizabeth gasped. How could so much have happened in only the few hours since dawn? But Robert was safe once more. She shuddered at the thought of what might have been and clung to his soggy arm.

''What now?'' he asked, contriving a smile as he tried to force his insides to settle. ''I am a trifle damp, my love, but I will dry.''

''I was only thinking how dreadful it would have been for you to spend eternity alone at the bottom of that odious moat.''

''He would not have been alone,'' Armand assured her. ''Many bodies lie in our deep water. The Fox of Boisvert defended his château well in time past and his archers slew many who tried to cross this moat. It is said their spirits rise on the night of the winter equinox and once more march on the château.''

''Ghosts!''

''But of course,'' he told her proudly. ''So old a château accumulates many. There is in the North Tower a bricked-up room containing the remains of the Fox's third wife.''

"And on the terrace," Delphine added, "there is a stain that spreads and darkens on the seventeenth day of every April."

"The guest who drank the poisoned wine," Armand offered.

"The headless coachman."

"The betrayed maiden who leaped from the east balcony."

"No, no, that is the stain on the terrace."

"Ah, yes, but do not forget the black monk who stalks the *comte*'s gallery in the west wing."

Appalled, Elizabeth remembered the darker shadow that had moved behind her in the hallway outside Robert's room—but she had suspected that to be either Dupont or Gérard following her! Dear God, she could not spend another night in this haunted château!

"Robert," she said, "I am going back to England by the very next boat."

His arm went about her, pressing her to him. "They are quizzing you, love." But his hard-won smile grew anxious, and they walked back to the château in silence.

She could not return to England! Across that hell-born channel! No matter what happened to the Boisvert estate, Elizabeth must remain at his side. It had never occurred to him that she might wish to leave France . . . and him.

WHILE THE GIRLS waited for the men to change clothes, Elizabeth wandered about the Great Hall. A frisson ran through her as she found the vacant place on the wall where Gérard had removed the ancient broadsword. Delphine watched her for several minutes before she spoke.

"You must know," she began in a tone that brooked no argument, "even though Armand's treasure does not exist, all is not lost to Armand and me. It is only to make a necessary change in my plans. I have discussed this already with him while we were in the maze."

She faced Elizabeth abruptly, her face serious. "I am sorry," she said, "but I am going to marry your Robert. I pretend it is I who must have wealth, but can you see my Armand as a man of the streets? Though I have for him a great love, I know he has neither the wit nor the craft to make a way for himself. He has no useful skills. He could not drive a coach or care for a garden or even properly polish a pair of boots. For Armand's sake, I must wed your Englishman."

Elizabeth stared at her in silence for a long moment, coming to a momentous decision. "Not," she replied quietly, "if I can stop it." *And,* she thought, *I can.*

Robert appeared on the gallery above, waving at them to join him. "Come up," he called. "We meet for a council of war before facing the executors and that priest."

They assembled in Armand's chamber. It seemed the safest place to talk, for on no pretext would Étienne enter there. Delphine sat on the side of the bed, Elizabeth took the chair and the men stationed themselves by the door.

Elizabeth saw Armand cast an agonized glance at his Delphine. The men must have come to terms. But whatever Robert had told him no longer mattered. Elizabeth had made a decision of her own, and it was time to put an end to all their foolishness. Opening her battle-scarred hatbox, she took her bedraggled bonnet from it and handed it to Delphine.

"This is all I have in the world," she said. "I give it to you for a wedding present."

Delphine stared at the filthy, dilapidated hat.

"The pearls in the roses belonged to my great-grandmother. They are real and worth a fabulous sum," Elizabeth explained. "Now I trade them to you for my happiness with Robert."

"The devil you say!" exclaimed that gentleman, and she smiled at him lovingly.

"I consider it a bargain."

Delphine frankly gaped at her. "And . . . and the diamonds on the leaves?"

"They are glass, unfortunately," Elizabeth spread her hands in a deprecating manner. They had been speaking in French and words from her schoolgirl lessons popped into her mind. The diamonds, she had said, were *verre*, glass. *Vert—*

vair—verre! The words were pronounced nearly alike! Armand had struck again.

"Oh, dear God!" she whispered, her eyes resting on the silver box on Armand's dressing table—the box with the curiously thick lid and a *glass,* not *green* fox, on its top. What better hiding place than one in plain sight?

"Armand—" her voice quavered "—where did you get that box?"

He looked puzzled. "It was of my mother. A gift from my father. She used to keep his *billets,* his letters, inside tied with a black riband from his hair."

"Let me see it!" Elizabeth reached for the box with a trembling hand. She studied it, peering closely at the ornamental lid. It was decorated with a landscape scene, a pool edged about with twined vines and flowers, and rising from the water in the centre, a hillock on which sat the ubiquitous Boisvert fox, delicately carved in crystal.

Yes, a hairline crack showed where the hillock met the pond, as if the tiny island bearing the fox was an added separate piece. But did the lid come apart? She tried twisting it and detected a slight movement. To the left, always to the left. An icy finger of excitement tingled up her spine.

Taking a firm grip on the lower part of the lid, she grasped the fox's hillock and turned it to the left. Three turns, and the lid came apart in her hands—revealing, not the handful of loose gems she expected, but a tightly folded, yellowed paper.

"One of the letters of my father, no doubt," Armand said without much interest.

She unfolded the sheet carefully. Not a letter. She held a dog-eared page from a church Bible, recording the births and marriages of the year 1792 in the village of Boisvert.

Near the top was the marriage of Eugène de Boisvert and one Marie-Jeanne Brunot. The final notation, some nine months later, was of the birth to Marie-Jeanne of a son, to be christened Armand Eugène Aristide de Boisvert.

Elizabeth tried to speak and emitted a series of squeaks.

Armand took the page from her shaking hands and read it slowly. He read it again.

A change came over him. He grew inches taller as he threw back his head and straightened his shoulders, cloaked in an oddly fitting mantle of dignity.

"*Merci au bon Dieu,*" he whispered, raising his eyes to the ceiling and crossing himself.

He turned to Robert. "*Mon ami,* it seems it is I, not you, who am the Comte de Boisvert."

They stared at him in frozen silence as the meaning of his words sank in.

Then, "Thank God!" exclaimed Robert. He clapped Armand on the shoulder, nearly knocking him down. "I ought to strangle you! None of this need have happened! I have crossed that devil-spawned Channel for nothing!''

''Oh, dear,'' said Elizabeth, remembering the voyage, as her scattered wits returned. ''And now you must cross back!''

''Never!'' Robert declared. ''Never will I set foot on a ship again.''

Elizabeth started to speak, but decided this was not the time.

Armand collapsed in the chair, their old Armand once more, and Delphine bounded into his lap, shrieking with delight.

When he could, he began to talk. ''I see now how it must have happened. I knew my *grand-père* discovered the *affaire* of my father and mother and sent his son away to serve in the court of the king. He must have secretly married my mother before he left to be guillotined with the royal family and she would have been terrified to let it be known I was his legal son lest I be torn from her arms and executed like my father.''

He looked up at them, an incredulous joy lighting his face. ''It was to save my life that she allowed me to be thought a bastard. All these years and now, I have again my mother—and a father. Who would have thought so immense a fortune to be held on a scrap of paper . . . ?''

THE EXECUTORS were gone, the priest had married Armand to his Delphine, and Étienne would, in time, get over his shock.

Elizabeth and Robert found a secluded corner of the garden in which to celebrate in their own fashion. It was then that Robert announced he intended for them to reside in France.

"But I want to go *home*," she told him. "Robert, you cannot remain in France forever! There is nothing for you here now."

He stared at her. Did she not remember what that rocking, heaving, bilge-smelling sailboat did to him? No one who had not suffered seasickness could understand the gut-wrenching torture of one's stomach turning itself inside out, over and over!

"Nothing would induce me to undertake that horrendous voyage again!"

His heart sank at the expression of exasperated pity that flickered across her face. She did not actually call him a coward as Breckenridge had, but surely she must have thought it. And he was not a coward! Had he not challenged a murderous thug swinging an axe with only a wooden pole in his own hands? And fended off a madman with a broadsword using only that same stick of wood?

"Robert, you cannot still fear water," she said patiently. "You swam—really swam—out of that hideous moat. How can you be afraid of a little trip on a boat?"

"Little! On that packet it would be nine hours of hell!"

He was serious. Elizabeth looked deep into his troubled eyes, past the physical dread, and saw there self-doubt, and self-disgust. Robert perceived his fear as a flaw in his character. It dawned on her that she faced a shadow that would colour the rest of their lives. For his own peace of mind, he must conquer this mountain—or rather, sea—in his journey to complete manhood. He had to have the triumph of overcoming this last weakness if he was to gain a full measure of self-respect. She could not let him live the rest of his life concealing the gnawing acceptance of his own cowardice. She knew only one way to force him to stand up to his fear.

"Robert," she said, "I am returning to England, with or without you."

She retired to her chamber and awaited his decision.

When time passed and he did not come, she ventured cautiously out and down the stairs. In the hall, she encountered Armand wandering in circles in the centre of the stone-paved floor, lost in a happy daze.

Before she could stop herself, she demanded, "Have you seen Robert? Do you know where he is?"

"Robert?" Armand came to life briefly, his eyes still glazed with wonder. "I believe he is out-of-doors. The last time I saw him, he was standing by the moat, staring down into it. I cannot imagine why. Gérard is not there.''

Elizabeth thought she knew. Her Robert was in the throes of coming to grips with his inner fear. She almost rushed to join him. No. It was for him to face himself and become the man she wanted, and the man he needed to be. She returned to her chamber to wait.

Hours crawled by, and Robert did not appear. She could come to only one conclusion. He did not love her or he would brave even the English Channel. She must leave France—and him, as soon as she could book passage. She could not bear to remain on the same continent, knowing he did not return her passion. Only propinquity had drawn them together; she had been relegated to the passing fancy he had once mentioned. Something heavy, built of ice, shattered in her chest. So this was how it felt when one's heart was broken—cold, misery, despair, desolation—there had to be stronger words. She deplored her limited vocabulary. She needed a dictionary if she was to wallow properly in self-pity.

Someone tapped on her door, and the splintered pieces of her heart crashed together in a great bound—then dribbled to the floor about her feet. It was not Robert. Delphine entered, carrying the hatbox.

"We now have no need for your pearls," she said. Unshed tears glistened in her eyes. "But, oh, never will we forget that you would have given them to us." She threw her arms about Elizabeth impulsively and hugged her.

This was too much for Elizabeth, whose feelings of loss and despair overcame her at last. Her own unshed tears began to trickle down her cheeks, and she gulped.

Delphine drew back and stared. "Elizabeth! What can be the matter?"

The dam breached, Elizabeth's words poured out in a flood. She could not stay in France, she wanted only to go home, her life was over, she would dwindle away into a crotchety spinster and leave all she had to a society devoted to sinking every boat in the English Channel!

"I see," said Delphine. "That idiot English did not ask you to marry him."

"Oh, it is not that. He asked, but I want to go home and he will not leave France. He... he fears being seasick more than he loves me, and I will not settle for second place."

"No more should you. This calls for a plan most drastic, and Étienne is the one to help."

"Étienne!"

"He will arrange for your passage to England on the next packet. He will be pleased to be of service, and when Robert sees you are determined, he will come to what senses the man may have. You will see.''

ROBERT, HAGGARD, watched the preparations for Elizabeth's departure in silence, waging his personal inner war. He knew enough of Elizabeth by now to accept that she would not change her mind. He tried to harden his heart, calling her selfish and unfeeling, but he suspected she was right.

In London, his terror of the sea mattered not. A thing to be ragged about by his friends. Now seeing himself in her eyes, he realized that never would he feel a complete man with such a flaw in his character. He shrank from the role of a coward, but at the very thought of that billowing, rolling Channel, his stomach churned and gorge rose. He could not!

TWO DAYS LATER, Elizabeth stood at the stern of the packet, looking her last on the coast of France. Resolutely, she walked to the bow, for it was forward to England from now on. England—without Robert. She could not believe how short a while she really had been gone. It seemed a lifetime!

London—Almack's and Vauxhall would still be there, but she couldn't have cared less. Covent Garden, Carlton House, Hyde Park... How strange that the famous names no longer evoked a response when she knew she would not visit them with Robert.

She tried to think of something else and wondered if Andrew was doing well in Vienna. She found she really didn't care, but she hoped Mayhew had made it safely home. In spite of her rigid resolve, tears of despair trickled down her cheeks. Robert had failed to master himself.

A small sloop caught up with the packet, bringing a late passenger but with her face buried in her handkerchief, she did not see...until a voice croaked behind her.

"Elizabeth?"

Never had she known a more beautiful sight than that wan, green countenance!

"Elizabeth, tell me quickly, if I live to reach England, which I doubt, will you marry me?"

There was no need to answer such an idiotic question. She steered him to the side.

"You will never see Italy or France for a honeymoon," he gasped, draping himself over the rail. "You cannot expect that of me."

She patted his back, but gently. "No, no, I never wish to leave England again."

"I'll kiss you," he choked, coming up for air, "after we reach land."

It would be soon enough for Elizabeth. She spread her new cloak, the parting gift of the new

Comte and Comtesse de Boisvert, over Robert's shoulders and prepared for the difficult trip, her heart singing a paean of joy.

Greater love, she knew, hath no man than this. With a tender smile, she watched him hanging over the rail.

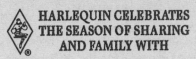

Relive the romance...
Harlequin and Silhouette
are proud to present

by Request™

A program of collections of three complete novels by the most
requested authors with the most requested themes. Be sure to
look for one volume each month with three complete novels by
top name authors.

In June: **NINE MONTHS** Penny Jordan
Stella Cameron
Janice Kaiser

**Three women pregnant and alone. But a lot can
happen in nine months!**

In July: **DADDY'S
HOME** Kristin James
Naomi Horton
Mary Lynn Baxter

**Daddy's Home... and his presence is long
overdue!**

In August: **FORGOTTEN
PAST** Barbara Kaye
Pamela Browning
Nancy Martin

**Do you dare to create a future if you've forgotten
the past?**

Available at your favorite retail outlet.

REQ-G

Harlequin is proud to present our best authors and their best books. Always the best for your reading pleasure!

Throughout 1993, Harlequin will bring you exciting books by some of the top names in contemporary romance!

In August, look for *Heat Wave* by

BARBARA DELINSKY

A heat wave hangs over the city....

Caroline Cooper is hot. And after dealing with crises all day, she is frustrated. But throwing open her windows to catch the night breeze does little to solve her problems. Directly across the courtyard she catches sight of a man who inspires steamy and unsettling thoughts....

Driven onto his fire escape by the sweltering heat, lawyer Brendan Carr is weaving fantasies, too—around gorgeous Caroline. Fantasies that build as the days and nights go by.

Will Caroline and Brendan dare cross the dangerous line between fantasy and reality?

Find out in HEAT WAVE by Barbara Delinsky... wherever Harlequin books are sold.

Fifty red-blooded, white-hot, true-blue hunks from every State in the Union!

Beginning in May, look for MEN MADE IN AMERICA! Written by some of our most popular authors, these stories feature fifty of the strongest, sexiest men, each from a different state in the union!

Two titles available every other month at your favorite retail outlet.

In September, look for:

DECEPTIONS by Annette Broadrick (California)
STORMWALKER by Dallas Schulze (Colorado)

In November, look for:

STRAIGHT FROM THE HEART by Barbara Delinsky (Connecticut)
AUTHOR'S CHOICE by Elizabeth August (Delaware)

You won't be able to resist MEN MADE IN AMERICA!